Bur

Al looked at Lodge[...] better tell them the [...] story," he said.

Lodgepoole sighed. "You've heard of the Bureau of Lost, right? Well, there's a second Bureau: the Bureau of Missing."

"Isn't that the same thing?" Simon asked.

"No. *Lost* refers to items. *Missing* refers to persons."

"You mean there are drawers full of missing *people* down there, too?"

"Not drawers, cryogenic chambers. Each equipped to keep the individual on ice for—well—forever. But we've had a slight problem . . ." He wrung his hands together. "A couple of the cryogenic cannisters unfroze, and the missing persons have escaped!"

Books available in the EERIE INDIANA series

All EERIE INDIANA titles can be ordered at your local bookshop or are available by post from Book Service by Post (tel: 01624 675137)

Eerie Indiana

Bureau of Lost

John Peel

MACMILLAN CHILDREN'S BOOKS

First published 1997 by Avon Books, USA
a division of The Hearst Corporation

This edition published 1999 by Macmillan Children's Books
a division of Macmillan Publishers Limited
25 Eccleston Place, London SW1W 9NF
and Basingstoke

Associated companies throughout the world

ISBN 0 330 37068 5

A CIP catalogue record for this book is available
from the British Library

Printed and bound in Great Britain by Mackays of Chatham plc, Kent

PROLOGUE

My name is Marshall Teller. Not too long ago, I was living in New Jersey, just across the river from New York City. It was crowded, polluted, and full of crime. I loved it. But my parents wanted a better life for my sister and me. So we moved to a place so wholesome, so squeaky clean, so ordinary that you could only find it on TV: Eerie, Indiana.

It's the American Dream come true, right? Wrong. Sure, my new hometown *looks* normal enough. But look again. Underneath, it's crawling with strange stuff. Item: Elvis lives on my paper route. Item: Bigfoot eats out of my trash. Item: I see unexplained flashing lights in the sky at least once a week. No one believes me,

1

but Eerie is the center of weirdness for the entire planet.

Since I moved here, I've started to think in a whole new way. Things that used to surprise me don't anymore. And if anything normal happens, I practically jump out of my skin. Like for example, if the neighbor's cat were to suddenly start barking, I wouldn't give it a second thought. But if I walked past their house and the cat meowed and rubbed up against my leg, I'd definitely wonder what was going on. When I reach into my coat pockets I expect to find someone else's gloves now. If I were to find both of my own, I'd be seriously freaked out. And nobody but me seems to have noticed how turned around everything in Eerie is.

At least, nobody except my friend Simon Holmes. Simon's my next-door neighbor. He's lived in Eerie his whole life, and he's the only other person who knows just how freaky this place is. Together, we've been keeping a record of all the stuff that happens around here. We've faced some of Eerie's most bizarre inhabitants and lived to tell about it, from the talking dogs that tried to take over the city to the crazy gray-haired kid who lives in the old abandoned mill and can't remember who he is. I told you this place was weird.

Still don't believe me? You will.

1

The two of us were in the Secret Spot. Okay, so it's just my attic, but that's where Simon and I go to discuss all the evidence we've collected about Eerie. Also, sometimes we just hang out there. Early that Saturday morning we were working on a jigsaw puzzle. It was a picture of a store called World of Stuff. The cool thing about World of Stuff is that you can get anything you want there. It's the ultimate in one-stop shopping. Mr. Radford, the owner, makes sure that the store is always stocked with pretty much everything from ice cream to comic books.

The jigsaw puzzle was Mr. Radford's latest promotional idea. Grinning wildly, he had given me one as a free sample. "It'll sell like hotcakes," he'd claimed. "Not that our hotcakes sell all that well," he admitted. "Well, it'll sell *better* than hotcakes!"

The picture on the puzzle showed stacked shelves, the booths where Simon and I sat to eat our ice-cream sundaes, and some racks of clothes. Mr. Radford was standing behind the counter, beaming, and his face took up about a third of the puzzle. It looked weird divided by the zigzagging lines that separated the pieces, but that's not what was bothering me. It was an easy puzzle. But it wasn't until Simon held the last two pieces in his hand and I saw the spaces where I'd fit them in that it finally hit me. This was no ordinary puzzle. *This kind of thing isn't supposed to happen here,* I thought. *Not in Eerie.*

I held out my hand. "Hand them over," I said.

"Okay." Simon dropped the pieces into my palm.

I eyed them in disbelief. "What's going on here?" I asked.

Simon's eyes widened. "Maybe one's from a different puzzle," he suggested, peering over my shoulder.

But when I placed the pieces neatly into their spaces, completing the puzzle, his face paled.

"I don't believe it." I stared at the assembled jigsaw. "All of the pieces are there. I've actually *finished* the puzzle."

"An unprecedented event," Simon agreed.

Anywhere other than in Eerie, finishing a jigsaw would be no big deal. But in Eerie, nothing is that simple. Neither of us had ever finished a jigsaw puzzle within the town limits. There was always at least one, and sometimes two, pieces missing.

And now . . . this!

"Weird," I said. "I think Lodgepoole must be slacking off on his job."

"You think so?" Simon glanced down at the puzzle again. His gaze wandered across the floor. Suddenly he gasped. "You're wearing matching socks!" he exclaimed.

I looked down and saw that he was right. I was wearing two dark blue socks. I guess I should explain that matching socks, like completing a puzzle, is another event that just never happens in Eerie. "Maybe he's sick," I mused.

Lodgepoole was one of the strangest

people that I had ever met. And, for Eerie, that was saying a lot. He had once run the Eerie branch of the Bureau of Lost. The Bureau sends out Certified Misappropriation Engineers to remove certain items—such as puzzle pieces and matching socks—from everyday life. Most of the things people think are lost have actually just been confiscated by the Bureau.

Of course, there are branches of the Bureau of Lost in every town in the world, at least according to Lodgepoole. But the Eerie division is much more thorough than the others. And that's because Lodgepoole is a very thorough kind of guy.

Simon and I knew that Lodgepoole's office was somewhere in Eerie, somewhere below ground. We'd both been there and seen the enormous rooms filled with missing items, all labeled LOST.

When we'd been there last, we'd also met Lodgepoole's assistant, Al. While Lodgepoole oversaw the entire division, it was Al's job to actually go out and retrieve the Lost items. But when the Head Office found out about some mistakes Lodgepoole had made, they demoted him and promoted Al.

Now Al ran the Bureau, and Lodgepoole was forced to do the dirty work—acquiring people's stuff.

At least, that's what he was *supposed* to be doing.

But I had *finished* a puzzle! *And* I was wearing matching socks. I shook my head. It was hard to imagine that Lodgepoole could have overlooked even one puzzle. But a puzzle and a pair of socks?

"Something's definitely wrong with Lodgepoole," I said.

Simon nodded gravely in agreement. "So what are we going to do?" he asked.

I headed for the door. "The only thing we can do," I said.

"Sundaes at World of Stuff?"

"Right. If we're going to get to the bottom of this, we're going to need brain food," I answered.

We each put on a pair of mirrored sunglasses and hopped on our bikes. Then we pedaled across Eerie toward the store.

I braked outside World of Stuff and propped my bike up against the front window. Simon pulled up behind me and hopped off his bike. As we opened the door to the store, a bell rang, alerting Mr. Radford to our presence.

"Ah, boys!" he called out, his moustache bristling as he smiled. "Did you finish the puzzle?"

"Yeah," I said. "It's a cool picture, Mr. R. Could we have a couple of hot fudge sundaes?"

"Coming right up." Mr. Radford bustled around behind the counter. "Yessiree, I think that jigsaw's going to be a hot item. I'm thinking of following it up with other scenic views of the town. The town hall. The police station. The dump . . . Why, the possibilities are endless!"

"Right," I agreed, wondering what kind of person would want to buy a jigsaw puzzle of the Eerie dump. On the other hand, in Eerie, there was no predicting what might be a hot seller. *Gone With the Wind* had been the best-selling book at the local bookstore for the past fifty years. Seventy-eight thousand copies of the book had been sold. And since there were less than seven thousand people in Eerie, and Eerie's not exactly a tourist spot, it was hard to guess who had bought all of them.

Simon and I sat down at one of the booths and Mr. Radford brought us our sundaes. I plunged my spoon into the mound of ice cream and fudge, and I could feel my brain clicking into gear. "Maybe we should look for Lodgepoole," I suggested between mouthfuls.

"What if *he's* Lost?" Simon argued.

"Then that will be another clue," I replied. "We both know what he looks like, and where he usually operates. Why don't we split up and scour the town?"

"Okay," Simon agreed. "Just as soon as we finish these." He swirled his spoon around in the bottom of the ice-cream dish.

Ten minutes later we checked that our walkie-talkies were working, and then sped off in opposite directions. Simon was checking the laundromat—one of the best places in town to lose things—and the bus depot. I was looking into the police station and the banks. Pens were *always* missing from there. But when there was no sign of any activity in either spot, I called Simon to report my failure.

"Nothing here, either," Simon's voice

crackled back over the radio. "Lodgepoole really is missing."

"Well, let's not give up," I replied. "Why don't you check the lockers at school? I'll check the chamber of commerce." I signed off and rode across to the chamber's office. Once there, I slipped my mirrored sunglasses into my pocket and walked through the door. There was a bulletin board inside, and Lodgepoole liked to confiscate a few notes each day. But today the board was more crowded with messages than I'd ever seen it. *Seriously weird*, I thought.

When I checked in with Simon, he reported that there was no sign of Lodgepoole at the school.

Something was *very* wrong.

I was about to head back to World of Stuff for another brainstorming session with Simon when I spotted a couple of huddled figures in the alley next to the chamber of commerce. They were obviously bums of some kind, wrapped in blankets. They were passing a bottle in a brown paper bag back and forth between them and taking turns drinking from it.

I'd never seen a homeless person in Eerie before. Let's face it: You need to be in good condition to deal with all the weirdness that goes on in this town. Homeless people are probably scared away from here pretty quickly. I inched closer to the men and watched them for a moment. One of them was wearing a green visor, and there was only one person I'd ever seen wearing one like it.

I stepped into the alley but the two men didn't seem to see me. I moved forward slowly and soon was only a few feet away from them.

One of the men took a long swig from the bottle. I looked down and recognized the red and yellow bottle cap of my favorite brand of root beer lying at my feet. The drinking man was tall and lean. His face looked tired and sad. He was wearing a green and blue scarf around his neck, a pinstriped shirt, a gold watch, and a large key on a chain around his neck. For a homeless person, he'd done pretty well. The other man was smaller and rounder, with gray hair and glasses that made him look like a depressed owl.

In an instant, I realized who I was looking at.

"Al!" I said to the man with the bottle. "Mr. Lodgepoole!" I added, turning to the shorter man. "What are you doing up here? Why aren't things getting lost?"

Al glanced up at me and blinked. "Oh, hi, kid," he mumbled in his gravelly voice.

"Teller, Marshall," Lodgepoole recalled. "History book, drawer, briefcase . . ." He was referring to the first time I'd met him after he'd confiscated my father's briefcase. He shook his head. "It's no use," he replied. "We're not working because we've lost it."

"Lost it?" I repeated. "Lost *what*?"

"Everything," Al answered.

I sighed, and pulled out my walkie-talkie. "Simon," I said. "I've found them. Meet me in the alley by the chamber of commerce."

"What's going on?" Simon asked.

"I don't know yet. They're not making a lot of sense." I signed off and stared at the two guys. They looked pretty depressed. "*What* have you lost?" I tried again.

"Everything," Lodgepoole repeated. "We've lost the Bureau of Lost."

2

I stared at him in amazement. "How can you lose a whole Bureau? That must be almost impossible."

"If we'd been trying," Lodgepoole said glumly, "it would have been a wonderful achievement. But we weren't, so it isn't." He took the root beer from Al and drank another sip.

"In fact, it's a catastrophe," Al added, snatching back the bottle. "And we're getting low on root beer, too. What a day."

It didn't seem as though I was going to get much more out of them, so I walked to the end of the alley and waited impatiently for Simon.

"Wow," he exclaimed as soon as he arrived and saw Lodgepoole and Al. "They look terrible!"

"I'm glad *somebody* appreciates our problem," Lodgepoole said. "We are miserable. Left without a place to lay our heads. Severed from the only home we know."

I sighed. "They've been going on like this for half an hour," I complained. "But they won't tell me what's going on. Just that they've Lost the Bureau of Lost."

"Isn't that kind of a big thing to misplace?" Simon asked.

"It's *not* misplaced," Al growled. "It's where it always was. We're not that clumsy."

This was making less and less sense to me. "If it's where it always was," I said patiently, "then how can you say you've lost it? Can't you just get back by crawling inside dryer number seven at the laundromat? That's what you used to do." There were secret entrances to the Bureau of Lost all over town, and Simon and I had discovered the one at the laundromat.

Al shook his head at Lodgepoole. "This kid doesn't know what he's talking about. He has no idea what kind of trouble we're in." He turned to me and sighed. "We can't get back that way. *They'll* be watching it," he said.

I took in the dark circles under the men's eyes. Lodgepoole's eyes were red, as if he'd been crying. "I think we're finally starting to get somewhere," I said. "You haven't misplaced the Bureau. You've been kicked out."

"Wow," said Simon. "Given your pink slips, huh? Poor guys."

"Fired?" Lodgepoole looked incensed. "*Us?* The best workers in the entire Bureau? I should think not! The very idea!"

"So, what happened?" I asked. "A hostile takeover by the Japanese or something?"

Al shrugged. "We can't talk about it. It involves a trade secret."

"We already know some of your trade secrets," I pointed out. "We know about the Certified Misappropriation Engineers who collect people's stuff, and the storage rooms at the Bureau where you store everything, and the Bureau's theory of economic growth." According to the Bureau of Lost, the best way to ensure economic growth in Eerie was for things to keep disappearing. That way, people would have to go out and buy new things to replace the old stuff.

Lodgepoole shook his head. "But this is a

different trade secret. It has nothing to do with that."

"This is a secret you really won't talk about," Simon said.

"Correct." Lodgepoole blinked away a tear. "The Bureau was my home for fifty years. To be evicted like this . . . It's more than the spirit can stand."

I frowned. "They can't just fire you after all this time. Was this eviction legal?" I asked.

Al bristled at the idea. "Certainly not!"

"Then why don't you think about a way of evicting *them,* instead of just sitting around here feeling sorry for yourselves?"

Sighing, Lodgepoole shook his head. "Don't you think that was the first idea we had?" he said. "But it's physically impossible for us, I'm afraid." He patted his stomach. "Too many years of eating well. One thing I've never been able to lose is weight. Still, if we're out in this alley long enough, I'm sure we'll starve down to size in a few weeks."

"By which time we'll have lost our jobs for certain," Al pointed out. If Head Office finds out what happened, we're done for."

He glared at me and Simon. "So, if you don't mind, we'd like to be left in peace. Beat it, kids."

They were obviously feeling too sorry for themselves to be polite. I shrugged. "Come on, kid," I said to Simon. "I guess there's not much more for us to do here."

"Kid?" Lodgepoole repeated. Then he looked at the two of us as if he were seeing some rare animal species for the very first time in his life. "You're just kids!" he exclaimed, almost happily. "Al, look at them!"

They must really be losing it now, I thought. I started to walk away, with Simon following close behind me, but Lodgepoole leaped to his feet, blocking our path.

"Hold on!" he exclaimed.

I eyed him in apprehension. "Let's make a break for it," I whispered to Simon. "Lodgepoole has cracked under all the strain."

But Lodgepoole must have overheard. "No," he said. "I haven't cracked yet. It's just that I've had the perfect idea of how to get the Bureau back. And you two are exactly the right size! Al, don't you agree?"

The other man stared at us, a smile breaking across his face. "Absolutely," he said. He rose to his feet, and the blanket he'd been wrapped in slid off his shoulders. He gazed down at Simon and me. "*Exactly* the right size."

"Boys," Lodgepoole said cheerily, "how would you like to do us a favor? Help us get our home back?"

I looked at him suspiciously. "On one condition," I replied. "You have to explain what's going on."

"It's a trade secret," Al said immediately.

"Al," Lodgepoole argued, "this is an emergency. And since this pair already knows one trade secret, we probably wouldn't get into too much trouble if we tell them another one."

Al considered the point for a moment. "I suppose not," he finally agreed. He gazed at the empty root beer bottle in his hand and then tossed it into a nearby Dumpster. "Okay, go ahead. You might as well tell them the whole story."

Lodgepoole turned to me and Simon. "You know that the Bureau of Lost is very large, right? Well, there's a second Bureau attached to it: the Bureau of Missing."

"Isn't that the same thing?" Simon asked.

"No," Lodgepoole said severely. "*Lost* refers to items. *Missing* refers to persons."

"Bureau of Missing," I said slowly, "as in missing persons. You mean there are drawers full of missing people down there, too?"

"Not drawers," Lodgepoole corrected me. "Cryogenic chambers. Each equipped to keep the individual comfortably on ice for—well—forever."

Simon shuddered. "That sounds pretty sick to me."

"It's not our idea," Al explained. "We don't make policy decisions. We're just the workers. If we're told that somebody's got to go Missing, then we snatch them and store them away. The place has been in operation for the longest time. It was there when we took over the Bureau. We just keep it going and add a few new people from time to time."

"So there's a big warehouse filled with frozen people?" I asked, to make sure I'd understood.

"Correct," Lodgepoole said. "And as long

as the units are working, the Missing People are kept on ice. But we've had a slight problem. . . ." He wrung his hands together. "A lot of the wiring is pretty old. Well, you've been down there. You've seen the place. Do you remember?"

It was hard to forget. Lightbulbs were hung across the ceiling of the underground chambers, but a lot of them had burned out and the place was dark and creepy. "Couldn't you use some of the Lost stuff to replace the broken stuff with?" I asked.

Lodgepoole jumped back as if I'd hit him across the face. "*Use* it?" he gasped. "But then it would no longer be Lost, would it? No, young man, the Lost stays Lost. What we did was put in requests for repairs."

"Four hundred and seventy-nine of them," Al added. "But who's counting?"

"It doesn't sound like the management's too concerned with upkeep," I offered.

"Precisely my point, too," agreed Lodgepoole. "Anyway, this morning we had a brownout."

"A what?" asked Simon.

"A power failure," Al explained. "Our power company's not the most reliable, either. They get their stuff from geothermal energy, and every time a volcano blows its top, it fries the power lines."

"Right," Lodgepoole said. "And when the brownout occurred, a couple of the cryogenic cannisters unfroze, and a couple of missing persons escaped."

"It happens from time to time," Al added. "Usually it's no big deal. When people get out they just wander around a bit until we spot them. We have them tagged so we can track them if they get out. We usually have them back before they're even seen by anyone."

"But that didn't happen this time," I said, finally catching on.

"It didn't," Lodgepoole agreed. "These two individuals are rather . . . agressive. And they had weapons. They struck while we were on our lunch break. Luckily, we spotted them before they could use their guns in a hostile fashion. We hid out."

"And then they started freeing some of the other Missing People," Al added. "There's quite a bunch of them down there now, and several of them have guns."

Simon held up his hands. "Hey, guys,

we're just *kids*. I don't know what you've got in mind for us, but if it involves men with guns, we're out of here."

"Oh, no," Lodgepoole said hastily. "There's no need for you to go anywhere near them at all. Quite the contrary. You'll be perfectly safe, I assure you."

"So who are these missing people, anyway?" I demanded.

Lodgepoole and Al exchanged glances, and then Lodgepoole sighed. "The two . . . gentlemen in question are Butch Cassidy and the Sundance Kid."

I stared at him in astonishment. "Butch and Sundance?" I asked. "Weren't they killed in South America or something?"

"Oh, no," Lodgepoole assured me. "That was merely legend. In fact, they simply became Missing."

Simon joggled my elbow. "Who are these guys?" he asked.

I shook my head. "Simon, haven't you ever seen that movie? It's a classic Western."

"I don't like Westerns," Simon answered. "I like scary films."

I sighed. There are so many things Simon

doesn't know. But then, I have to remind myself that he's just a kid. "Butch Cassidy and the Sundance Kid are these two guys who went around robbing trains and holding up banks," I explained. "Then they ran for cover in South America, where they supposedly got into a big fight with the police in Bolivia and were killed."

"*Supposedly*," Lodgepoole said. "Nobody knows for sure, of course, which is how we like it to be. That keeps things interesting."

"They're very tough guys," I pointed out. "And used to a lot of violence." I was beginning to agree with Simon. Maybe this would be a good case to pass on. We could always get in touch with Lodgepoole later to find out what happened. We didn't have to be firsthand witnesses.

"I detest violence," Lodgepoole said. "I like order, calmness and a serene working environment. But at this very moment my office is being despoiled by those two ruffians and their accomplices. We *have to* get it back."

"But how, exactly, do you think you can get back in charge of the place?" I asked.

Al shrugged. "There's a lot you don't

know about the Bureau," he explained. "Like the Emergency Neutralization Plan. You see the Bureau has backup plans for everything that can possibly go wrong."

"Almost everything," I pointed out. "Otherwise you wouldn't be needing our help."

"Quite correct," Lodgepoole had to admit. "Well, the Bureau put the E.N.P. in about fifty years ago and . . . well, let's just say a whole lot of dentists suddenly found that they were missing their supplies of laughing gas. The cannisters of gas were installed in the Bureau, ready to be used in case of an emergency like this one. All Al and I would have to do is to get to two small computer controls and operate them at precisely the same instant."

"That's a fail-safe," Al added. "If it was just one control, it might happen during a brownout. Then it would be the two of us who'd get knocked out."

"Okay," I agreed. "I think I get the picture. Two computers have to be given passwords at the same time, and then the Bureau will be flooded with laughing gas. Then you two can clean up and put everybody back where they belong."

"That's it exactly," agreed Lodgepoole.

"So, where's the snag?" Simon asked brightly. "Why can't the two of you just do it?"

Lodgepoole and Al exchanged glances again and sighed. "Because," Lodgepoole finally explained, "we were very much younger when the system was installed. We've both grown and put on weight since then. I'm afraid we can't fit inside the access tubes anymore."

Finally I was beginning to understand. "So you need us to go into the tubes for you and switch on the gas release."

"Exactly," Al said. "We can take care of the rest from there. And with a little luck, Head Office won't even notice a thing, and we both get to keep our jobs."

I nodded thoughtfully, then glanced at Simon. He looked as freaked out as I was feeling. "We'll have to talk it over," I informed them.

Simon and I walked to the end of the alley and turned the corner so that we couldn't see or hear Lodgepoole and Al. "What do you think, Simon?" I asked.

"I don't know," Simon admitted. "It sounds cruel to me, locking people up forever. I don't know if I want to help them do that."

I felt exactly the same way. "On the other hand, Butch Cassidy and the Sundance Kid are pretty dangerous. If they're not locked up, they'll probably go on another robbing and shooting spree. And right now they have access to all the computer systems in the Bureau. They could get their hands on all kinds of stuff. I mean, Lodgepoole and Al are weird, but at least they know what they're doing."

"I don't know," Simon said. "I have a really bad feeling about this, but I guess we don't have much choice. We can't just leave the Bureau in the hands of criminals."

"Right," I said. "But as soon as we're up from below, we're out of here. Okay?"

"Okay," said Simon

We walked back into the alley. Al was leaning down, whispering sharply into Lodgepoole's ear, but when he saw us he broke away. Lodgepoole looked pale and shaky.

"Okay, we'll do it," I said.

Color flooded back into Lodgepoole's face immediately. He grabbed my hand and pumped it happily up and down. "Splendid, splendid! I knew we could count on you. There wasn't a doubt in my mind. I didn't even worry—not for one second."

"Um, yeah," added Al. "Thanks for helping us out. Tell you what—we'll give the two of you special treatment when this is all done. You'll never lose anything again, or at least, not on our account."

"Of course, that only applies *after* we get the Bureau back," Lodgepoole quickly explained. "So let's not lose any time. We should get started right away."

"How?" I asked.

Lodgepoole nodded his head briskly. "We're going to have to use the entrance in the back of Simon's closet. I think that should be perfect."

Simon's eyes opened wide. "There's an access to the Bureau of Lost right inside my closet? Wow, no wonder I'm always losing stuff."

"Never again," Al promised. "*If* this plan works."

"*If?*" I blinked. "I thought you said it was foolproof."

"It is," Lodgepoole said hastily. "Almost."

Somehow, that didn't make me feel any better about this whole thing. . . .

3

Since Simon's parents had both gone shopping, slipping Lodgepoole and Al into the house wasn't a problem. We hurried upstairs to Simon's room.

"I'll open it up," Al said. He disappeared into the back of the crowded closet, and I could hear him fiddling around inside, shoving Simon's shoes and toys to one side. A moment later he slid a square section of the back of the closet wall open like a sliding door. Simon and I peered through it. Two long firemen's poles disappeared into the darkness below.

"This is the bit I hate," Lodgepoole admitted, looking a little pale. "But that's only because I have a fear of heights. This first step's a big one. The two of you follow us down. The wall will close automatically in thirty seconds, so you don't have to worry about that." He swallowed nervously. "Just the drop. Just one little drop. Hold on tight." Then he rushed forward and grabbed onto the pole. He quickly dropped from view.

"See you in a minute," Al said as he followed Lodgepoole.

I felt a lump in my stomach. I guess I'm afraid of heights, too, especially when I'm jumping into something and I can't see the bottom where I'm going to land. Not that that's happened to me before.

"This is so cool," Simon said happily. "I never knew they were in there." He grabbed onto the lefthand pole, and I took the right. "This is just like *Mission Impossible!*"

And we both started to fall. In the darkness I picked up speed. I could barely make out Simon's figure on the pole opposite me. "They should install one of these rides in Disney World," I commented. Now that I had actually taken the plunge, my stomach was starting to feel a little bit better.

Suddenly the shaft went completely black

and I realized that the door above us must have slid shut. "And maybe they could wire up a few lightbulbs, too," I added. You could tell they didn't use this entrance very often!

Finally there was a faint glow from below us. It telescoped almost immediately into a brighter light, and then the shaft opened into a large room. A second later my feet hit a padded mat, and I let go of the pole. I heard a *thump* a few feet away from me, and I knew that Simon had landed also. I sat up dizzily and looked around.

We were in a small room deep underground. Like the rest of the Bureau, it looked as though it could stand to be soaked in detergent for a few hours. Huge dust balls carpeted the floor and cobwebs lined the ceiling. There were boxes scattered around the room, and a door leading out into a corridor. Lodgepoole and Al were waiting in the hallway, and I noticed that Lodgepoole looked a little green.

"This place needs dusting," I told them.

"We don't use it very often," Lodgepoole apologized.

"Actually, we've only used it once before—to test it when we first installed it," Al said. "It's kind of fun."

Lodgepoole shuddered.

"That was so cool. Let's do it again," Simon said enthusiastically.

"We've got better things to do with our time," Lodgepoole said sternly. "Come along, come along." He led the way down the short, narrow corridor to another, bigger room. On a table in the center of the room there was some kind of machine with gears and a conveyor belt. It looked like a weird old sewing machine, or something out of a monster movie.

"All you're missing is a monster under a sheet," I joked. "Er . . . You don't have one, do you?"

But Lodgepoole and Al just ignored me. Maybe they were feeling sensitive about how old all the Bureau's equipment was, which didn't make me feel too confident myself.

"All right, over here," Al said. He led the way to two huge vertical pipes, both maybe two feet wide. "These are the access points," he explained. "They'll be a bit cramped for you, but you should be fine. You just climb down the pipe along that ladder about twenty feet and then you'll each come to a cross-tunnel. You have to crawl along that. The Emergency Neutralization panels are at the end of each of the tunnels. When you reach the end, simultaneously activate the pair of them, and then return here."

"That's all?" I asked. "It sounds pretty easy."

"Hopefully, it will be," Lodgepoole said. "By the time you get back here, and we go down to the main floor, the gas will have cleared, so we'll be unaffected. But the Missing People should be all dazed and dreamy. Now, hurry along, hurry along."

"Okay," I agreed. "But we have to get ready first." I unslung my backpack, which would get caught on the descent if I kept it on, and removed a walkie-talkie. I always keep a spare radio, just in case something goes wrong, and this time I handed it to Al and Lodgepoole.

Simon had his own walkie-talkie, which he whipped out of his backpack and turned on.

"We use these to keep in touch," I explained. "And now you'll be able to hear how we're doing, and give us advice if there's a problem."

"What sort of a problem?" asked Lodgepoole.

"I don't know," I told him as patiently as I could. "If I knew now, then we wouldn't need the walkie-talkies. Okay, let's just test them." When we were sure they were all working I slung mine over one shoulder and turned to the access tubes.

Al fiddled with the latch and opened a glass door. I could see the rungs of a ladder leading downward. "Good luck, kid," he said.

"Thanks," I replied. "Hopefully we won't need it." I gripped the top rung and swung into the tube. "See you soon." I started to climb down.

Thankfully, the tube was lit, and I could see where I was going. Not that I looked down much—when I did, it looked as though the ladder stretched down forever. I realized that it would be an awfully long drop if I lost my grip. The thought made my palms all slippery and sweaty against the rungs of the metal ladder. I was pretty happy to finally reach the floor.

The cross-tunnel was right where Al had said it would be. I got off the ladder and got down on my hands and knees. There was no way an adult could have fit inside one of these. As it was, I would have to crawl on my stomach the entire way. I started down the tunnel. Light glittered off a long strip on the lefthand wall so I could see that the opening wasn't getting any bigger. If anything, it looked as though it would be a tighter fit further ahead.

I took a deep breath. Sometimes when I'm in the basement I wonder what would happen if there was an earthquake or a volcano or something. I'd be trapped underground. I decided that this wasn't a good time to think about that. I clutched my walkie-talkie and turned it on. "I'm in the cross-tunnel," I reported, "and making my way forward. How are you doing, Simon?"

"Fine," came his reply. "I'm in the side tunnel, too. It's kind of tight in here, but okay."

"All right," I said. "Keep in touch if

anything happens." I continued to move forward. To my right I noticed a shiny silver panel covered with buttons. One of them said *Emergency Neutralization Control.* "I've found a panel," I reported.

"That's the decoy," Al's voice crackled through the walkie-talkie.

"Decoy?" I asked, confused.

"There are *two* panels," Lodgepoole explained. "I thought we mentioned that. The first one is the decoy, just to keep the system out of the wrong hands. Whatever you do, don't touch it."

"Too late," I heard Simon say.

There was a sputter of protest from the handset, which finally resolved itself into Al's voice. "Kid, *don't* tell me you hit any of the buttons."

"Just the one marked *power,*" Simon answered. "Why? Is there a problem?"

There was a moment of silence, and then Lodgepoole said quietly, "You've just activated the defense mechanism. A laser beam will be fired from the *real* defense panel ahead of you in about . . . oh, thirty seconds."

"Thirty seconds?" I yelped, starting to

panic. "And you didn't think to tell us about this *before* we started?"

"It slipped my mind," Al grumbled. "So sue me."

If I'm alive in thirty seconds, I might, I thought. "Okay, how do we stop it?"

"Uh . . . There's no way to stop it. Twenty seconds." Al said nervously.

We needed something to deflect the beam, or reflect it. But neither Simon or I had mirrors!

"Marshall!" Simon sounded worried. "Do something!"

"Sunglasses!" I exclaimed. "Simon, use your mirrored sunglasses to reflect the beam!" I pulled my own from my pocket, holding them out in front of me. "Lodgepoole, do you think this will work?"

"Definitely," said Lodgepoole. "Unless . . ." his voice trailed off thoughtfully.

"Unless what?" Simon asked.

"Well, you know. Unless it doesn't," he replied.

In the background, I heard Al ask, "Do you think we'll be able to get the bodies out and get some other suckers to go down there next?"

Not exactly inspiring.

If my plan didn't work, Simon and I were going to be well-done steaks. . . .

There was a flash of light from down the tunnel and a buzzing sound. I almost screamed. My stomach hurt and my hands shook as I held up the sunglasses.

The laser beam struck the mirrored lenses. Then it jutted straight back down the tunnel.

It was working!

But the glasses were starting to get warm from the laser. Then warmer. First the glasses would melt, and then me!

A drop of liquid glass dripped down onto the floor of the tunnel. My fingers where they gripped the rims were starting to heat up painfully. Even if the lenses held up, I'd have to drop them pretty soon. Sweat was pouring off my brow but I held the glasses as steadily as I could in the path of the beam of light.

And then there was silence. The glasses in my hand were cooling off rapidly. The beam had shut off.

I dropped the glasses and shook my hands to cool them off. There were red burns across my fingertips. As soon as I could, I grabbed the walkie-talkie. "Simon!" I yelled. "Are you all right?"

There was no answer, and for a minute I held my breath. Finally his voice came out of the speaker. He sounded shaken up. "Yeah, I'm here, Marshall," he said. "I'm not sure if my fingers are, but the rest of me definitely is."

"Well, at least you're still alive," Al growled. "Now, get moving again. And this time don't touch anything unless we tell you to, okay?"

I sighed. "You could at least say that you're glad we're not french toast," I pointed out, but Al did not respond. I pushed the ruined glasses away from me and continued to crawl down the tunnel. As far as I was concerned, the sooner we were done with this case, the better. "We're doing all of this to help you. Out of the kindness of our hearts," I reminded them.

"Of course you are," Lodgepoole said. "And we do appreciate it. But please hurry. Setting off the laser defense will have registered in the main office. One of the escapees might have noticed it."

"Okay, okay." I crawled ahead for about another twenty feet, where the tunnel abruptly ended. In the wall ahead of me was another control panel. "I think I've reached the real one this time," I reported. "It's directly ahead of me."

"That's the one, kid," Al agreed. "Simon, have you reached yours yet?"

"Yeah," Simon answered. "I see it."

"Good," said Lodgepoole. "Now, follow my instructions very carefully. At the bottom of the panel on the left should be a bright red button."

I looked. "You mean the one marked *Do not touch. Danger?*"

"That's the one," Al radioed back. "Now, press it."

"What? Do you think I'm crazy?" I exclaimed. I wasn't about to take any more chances.

"It's the off switch for the panel's defenses," Al explained. "The warning's a fake."

"Has anyone ever told you guys that you're paranoid?" I said into the handset. I hoped they really did know what they were doing. Taking a deep breath, I pressed the button.

A light below it blinked on. It read: *Do not press that button again.*

"Wow!" said Simon's voice. "Let me guess, we do press it again?"

"No!" yelped Lodgepoole and Al at the same moment.

"This time, the warning's real," Al added. "It would start up the defenses again, and you'd both be history. Uh, you didn't press the button again, did you?"

"Of course not," Simon answered. "You told me not to touch anything unless you told me to."

"Good." The radio was silent for a minute. "At the top of the panel there are a row of buttons, all green. They're all marked *on*. See them?"

I checked. "There's five of them," I reported.

"Right. Now, press the second from the left."

"I thought it was the second from the right," Lodgepoole objected.

"That's on even-numbered days," I heard Al growl. "Today's the seventeenth."

"Actually," I said, trying to stay calm, "it's the sixteenth."

"Are you sure about that?" Al asked.

"Trust me," I answered. "I deliver newspapers. It's Saturday the sixteenth."

"Oh. Well, in that case, press the second from the right."

I crossed my fingers and pressed the button.

"Okay, now what?" Simon said over the radio.

"There's a handle on the right side of the panel. It should be pointing straight up."

I saw it.

"This is the critical part," Lodgepoole's voice instructed us. "Both of you must grip the levers and pull them down at the exact same moment. That will release the gas."

"Okay." I gripped my lever tightly. "Simon, are you set?"

"Ready," Simon said.

"On three," I told him. "One . . . two . . . *three*." I jerked down on the lever, which clicked smoothly into place. Nothing seemed to happen. "Uh, is that it, guys?" I called.

"That's it," Lodgepoole confirmed. "Now, the two of you just have to come back out here, and then we can go and take control of the Bureau again. Nicely done, boys."

"Thanks." I started to inch backward down the tunnel, since there was no room to turn around. I could only hope that Al and Lodgepoole had managed to get the instructions right. Otherwise the four of us could be walking right into a trap.

4

I was completely sick of enclosed spaces by the time I rejoined Lodgepoole and Al in the dusty room. A moment later, Simon popped his head out of his cylinder.

"That wasn't my idea of fun," he commented. A patch of his curly hair had gotten scorched by the laser beam. "I almost got broiled."

"You should learn to obey orders, then," Al grumbled.

I wanted to remind him that he had forgotten to give us the correct orders, but it seemed pointless. I mean, he was obviously just shaken up because of this whole mess.

"Let's go and see what's happened, shall we?" Lodgepoole said. He led the way down another corridor until, after about ten minutes of walking, we reached what looked like a bulkhead from a submarine. For all I knew, that's really what it was. There was a line of writing on it in what looked like Russian. Lodgepoole hesitated beside it.

"Aren't we going in?" Simon asked.

"Yes, of course," Lodgepoole answered. "It's just that I want to be absolutely certain that the gas has dissipated before we do. It wouldn't be a good idea to open the door and get knocked out, too."

"For all you know," I added, "the gas didn't even go off, and everyone's waiting inside with drawn guns."

That made Lodgepoole even paler. "Of course it went off," he insisted, a little uncertainly. "You followed the correct procedure, didn't you?"

"Yes," I replied. "But the system's never been tested, has it? And after all this time, it might have rusted up or something."

"The kid's got a point," Al said. He took several steps back. "I think that *you'd* better open the door," he told Lodgepoole, "and we'll wait back here. This way, if there *is* any gas present, then we can run for

48

cover. And if it didn't work, they'll only get one prisoner."

"Or target," I said.

"Why should *I* do it?" Lodgepoole squeaked.

"Because I'm the boss and I say so," Al answered, crossing his arms. "You wouldn't want one of the kids to do it, would you?"

Lodgepoole looked as if that was exactly what he wanted. But he swallowed nervously and took a step forward. He tapped a code into a panel next to the door. Then he grabbed the handle in the center of the door and spun it around before he could lose his courage. With a terrible squeaking sound, the door swung open. Lodgepoole stood still with his eyes shut.

When nothing happened, he gave a sigh of relief and opened his eyes again. "It's all right," he announced. "No laughing gas and no guns."

Al led Simon and me forward, and we entered the main section of the Bureau of Lost. Al swung the door shut behind us and fastened it again. "Let's get to the command center," he grunted, leading the way.

We passed along corridors and through rooms that were packed with all kinds of stuff. Two huge rooms were crammed with books. There was a room filled with papers, most of which looked like homework assignments. Barrels filled with pen tops, pencils, and other school supplies, like compasses and protractors, lined the walls. There were other barrels filled with erasers and staplers. Some of the rooms were filled with clothing, and others with balls of wool. And I even passed a huge freezer filled with Forever Ware containers.

In fact, the Bureau had at least one of everything: an old Mustang aircraft; a large yacht, flopped on its side; even a satellite in one of the larger rooms.

"This is a cool place," Simon said. "It would be great to explore it under different circumstances."

"The very idea!" Lodgepoole snapped. "You would probably wreak havoc on our inventory system. Please don't touch *anything*."

"Spoilsport," Simon muttered.

It was in a room filled with fishing rods and golf balls that we saw our first person.

It was a man in very old clothing, and he was fast asleep on the floor and snoring. Beside him lay an antique musket.

"One of the 'Roanokers,'" Al said. "Must have been a lookout. The gas got him good."

"Roanokers?" Simon asked. "What's that? And why's he dressed so funny?"

"Don't they teach you *anything* in school these days?" Lodgepoole said. "Roanoke was one of the earliest settlements in North America. It's an island off the coast of North Carolina. Between fifteen eighty-seven and fiteen ninety, all one hundred and seventeen people there vanished without a trace." He looked rather pleased with himself. "One of the Bureau's earliest efforts, and a total success."

"Well, don't just stand there talking," Al complained. "You'd better bring him with us. We can't leave him here."

Lodgepoole stared at him in disbelief. "You don't expect me to carry him, do you?"

"I don't care how you bring him, as long as you bring him," Al replied.

"Well, I've got a bad back," Lodgepoole

protested. "I can't possibly carry a man that size."

I decided I'd better head off their argument. "There's a wheelbarrow over here," I said. "Why don't we just lift him into that, and then you can push it?"

It took just a few moments, and then we were on our way again, Lodgepoole huffing and complaining about the work he was being forced to do.

Finally we reached the command center. Here was the big desk and the bank of TV monitors on which Al could see what was happening on the streets of Eerie and locate items that had to be Lost.

And here was the bulk of the Missing People. There had to be over a hundred of them, all fast asleep. Many were armed with guns, and others had swords or spears. Two Native Americans had bows and arrows.

"There are so many of them," Simon said in awe.

"We've been collecting them for quite some time," Lodgepoole said proudly.

"So now what?" I asked.

"We put them back, of course!" Lodgepoole exclaimed, looking at me as if I were mad. "What else?"

"Into suspended animation?" I asked. "Those cryogenic tubes of yours?"

"Naturally."

I shook my head. "Look, I don't mind helping you get the Bureau back again, but I think what you're doing to these people is cruel and unusual punishment. You should let them go."

"Let—them—go?" repeated Lodgepoole in astonishment. "Really! You have absolutely no idea what sort of chaos that would cause."

"Besides, kid," Al said, "a lot of these guys have been out of circulation for an awful long time. Think of the trouble they'd have getting adjusted to computers, cars, and cash machines. Not to mention fast food, in-line skating, and video games."

He had a point. Someone who had lived on Roanoke Island in the sixteenth century would hardly be able to cope with microwave popcorn, let alone cars and airplanes and the Internet. "But I think what you're doing to them is horrible."

"Kid, in most cases, we saved their lives.

They'd be dead by now if they hadn't become Missing Persons." He pointed to a man in arctic survival gear. "That's Captain Oates. He was on Scott's expedition to the south pole in 1911. He went out into a blizzard, willing to die to help his friends survive. Our Bureau brought him here. And those guys on Roanoke Island would have been massacred by the natives if we hadn't saved them."

"It still seems wrong," I said.

"That's a management decision," Lodgepoole pointed out. "You'd have to take up your complaint with them."

I opened my mouth to respond but Lodgepoole held up a hand.

"And nobody sees *them* without an appointment."

"Very few people see them even *with* an appointment," Al added. "But since you've both been so helpful, we'll put in a good word for you. In the meantime, we've got to get these guys back to their tubes before the gas wears off, otherwise we'll be in trouble again. So be good sports and lend a hand, okay?" He pointed to the various guns. "Or do you want to just hang around and let them shoot you?"

I sighed and glanced at my watch. It was past lunchtime. I was hungry and my burned fingers were really starting to hurt. Right then my first priority was getting out of this mess. But it seemed like the only way I was going to do that was to go along with their plan.

"Relax, kid," Al assured me. "When you talk to the Bureau they'll explain everything."

I nodded. "Okay," I said. "Let's just get this over with."

Simon and I helped Lodgepoole and Al load the sleeping bodies into wheelbarrows. Then we lugged them to the cryogenic chamber, where the bodies would be kept in storage.

"Creepy," Simon remarked as we entered a huge room filled with upright metal boxes. Narrow tubes protruded from the top of each of the boxes and met at a central control panel in the middle of the room.

"Like a graveyard for the undead," I agreed. The boxes definitely reminded me of coffins or tombstones. And there was a plaque with a name on it at the bottom of each one.

By the time we'd brought all the bodies back to the coffins, I was exhausted and extremely freaked. I glanced at Simon and noticed a drop of sweat rolling down his cheek. I'd put a lot of bodies into their boxes. And a lot of them were famous people I'd learned about in school or read about in books, like Glenn Miller and Amelia Earhart.

As Simon and I dragged in the sleeping bodies, Lodgepoole and Al closed the boxes and turned the controls to deep freeze. Finally all the bodies were locked in.

I turned to Simon. "Great job," I said. "Now let's get out of here."

"Not so fast," Al said. "We're missing some bodies." He pointed to a few empty boxes at the far end of the the room.

"Where could these guys be?" asked Simon. "We got everyone. I checked all the rooms, the hallways, everywhere."

"Kids, this is the computer age," Lodgepoole said. "We don't have to run all over the place peering around corners and checking corridors. We'll simply consult the main computer."

We followed him into the command center. He walked over to the computer desk and flicked the switch to *on*. The screen lit up and a map of the Bureau of Lost appeared. Lodgepoole tapped several buttons, and the screen suddenly zoomed in on a few of the rooms in the map. Lights came on in two of the rooms. Most of them were in the Missing People room, all blinking green. Four lights blinked red in the command center.

There were no other lights at all.

"I don't get it," Simon admitted. "We're in there. And the undead guys are in there. But where are the missing Missing People?"

"Most likely a computer glitch," Lodge-poole said with a catch in his voice. "Nothing to worry about, I'm sure. We'll have it working again in no time."

"But what if the computer is right?" I asked, my voice rising. "What if the missing Missing People aren't in the Bureau at all?"

"Not in the Bureau?" Lodgepoole asked.

"The kid is right," Al said. "They must

have gone upstairs and out. To Eerie. They're probably loose up there right now."

I felt a lump rise in my throat. I had a feeling things were about to get a whole lot worse.

"Well, at least we know who we're dealing with," Lodgepoole announced. "The five empty boxes belong to Butch Cassidy, the Sundance Kid, Jesse James, D.B. Cooper, and Captain Vanderdecken. So that's a start, right?" he added.

"Sure," Simon answered glumly. "Great."

Al sat down quickly in a chair at the computer table. "We'll have to proceed with the utmost caution," he said. "These men are armed and dangerous."

"They'll also be disoriented, angry, and desperate," Lodgepoole pointed out. "Don't forget that."

Simon and I groaned. "How can we?" I said.

5

"So, do you guys have any kind of backup plan?" I asked.

"In case the Missing People have gotten out into the town," Simon explained.

Lodgepoole and Al just looked at each other.

I figured that meant the answer was no. The lump in my throat was growing, but I couldn't let it get me down. There was too much we had to do. "Let's get a move on it, then," I said. "They can't have been gone long, can they? And they're bound to be really conspicuous, aren't they?"

Al started to look hopeful. "The kid's got a point," he admitted. "If we can just track them down and tranquilize them, we can bring them back here. We have that tranquilizer gun we used last year to round up the missing rats from the Eerie Laboratory."

"You used tranquilizer darts on rats?" I asked.

"I didn't want to alarm them," Lodgepoole explained. "This way they slept through the entire move. When they woke up they were home, safe and sound at the Bureau."

"But will these darts be strong enough to work on people?" Simon asked.

"Oh they're wonderful," Lodgepoole said. "I use them myself sometimes when I have trouble sleeping."

I wondered if the darts had done some kind of long-term damage to Lodgepoole's brain. But I had to admit that he seemed about as normal as the rest of the Eerie population—which wasn't saying much, of course.

But while Lodgepoole and I were talking, Simon had gone to check out the empty cryogenic boxes.

"There's a box for someone named Elvis Presley," he said. "Who's that?"

"Looks like he's been gone for a while," I

said. The inside of the box was covered with huge gobs of dust.

Lodgepoole went white, and Al shook his head. "We don't talk about *him*," Al said. "He got away almost as soon as he arrived. He's constantly being spotted all over the country, but we've never managed to track him down. He's obviously in hiding far from Eerie. I don't think we need to worry about him right now."

I thought of mentioning the Elvis look-alike on my paper route, but I figured it would just upset them more. "So there are five people to get back," I said. "That's not too bad, is it?"

"You wish," Lodgepoole muttered. "Those five are among the most dangerous people around. Catching them again won't be easy."

"Who are they?" asked Simon. "I mean, you told me about Butch Cassidy and the Sundance Kid, but what about the other three?"

"Jesse James is another outlaw from the old West," Lodgepoole explained.

I frowned. "I thought he was shot in the back," I said. "There's a song about 'the dirty little coward, who shot Mr. Howard.'"

Lodgepoole shook his head. "That was just a cover-up," he answered. "In fact, the supposed killer was one of his gang, and the thing was staged so that Jesse could disappear."

"Yes," Al agreed with a wide grin. "Only the Bureau made him disappear a bit further than he had intended."

"What about the Captain?" I asked.

"Vanderdecken," Al said. "Better known as the 'Flying Dutchman.' He was a sea captain who was supposed to have been doomed to wander the seven seas forever, never putting into port. But eventually he just seemed to fade away. Well, that's because we've got him here."

"We *had* him," Lodgepoole pointed out. "And now he's loose upstairs somewhere."

"And that last guy?" I persisted.

"D.B. Cooper?" Lodgepoole sighed. "An airline hijacker. In the seventies, he hijacked a plane and demanded a two-hundred-thousand-dollar ransom. Then he jumped out of the plane with a parachute and was never seen again."

"And we can guess why," I answered. "So

these are just five guys. And they're probably so confused they don't even know what hit them." At least, I hoped they were confused.

Because they weren't just any five Missing People. They were all criminals, and by the sound of things, pretty ruthless ones at that.

Simon, Al, and Lodgepoole were all staring at me. "Okay," I conceded, "it could be trouble."

"Yes," Lodgepoole answered. "But each of them has a small device planted in his shoe, just in case of emergency. So at least we'll be able to track them."

Al crossed to the wall and opened a large gun case. "And then let them have it," he added, taking out two large rifles.

"You're going to *kill* them?" gasped Simon.

"No, of course not," Al answered. "I just finished telling you. These shoot tranquilizer darts. The sort of things zookeepers use to knock out animals. Scientists use them to knock out rodents. Beekeepers use them to knock out bees. You know, that sort of thing. So all we have to do is to hit them with a dart, and they keel over, fast asleep." He handed one rifle to Lodgepoole and kept the other himself.

"Um, maybe Simon and I should be the ones to hold the guns," I suggested. "No offense or anything," I added.

Al glared at me. "Please," he said. "Lodgepoole and I are professionals. And now, all we need are the trackers." He took what looked like two small remote control units out of the desk drawer and handed one to Lodgepoole. Each unit was the size of a small calculator and had a single readout on it with an arrow. "These point right at the tracking devices," he explained. "Once we get upstairs, all we have to do is switch them on and then follow the arrows."

"Then we'd better get on with it," Lodgepoole suggested, "before management realizes we've lost people." He led the way over to an elevator in the corner of the room. Scowling, he turned back to Simon and me. "And you'd better forget all about the secret entrance in Simon's closet," he warned us. "It's not for joyrides."

"Relax," I said. "I don't think either one

of us is going to want to pay another visit to this place."

Simon nodded. "Yeah," he said. "From now on I won't even go near my closet. Believe me."

We got into the elevator, and Lodgepoole closed the doors. "Hold on," he cautioned, and then hit the top button.

The elevator started upward with a jolt. I stumbled and grabbed onto the railing. Simon lurched forward and then caught hold of my arm.

"Neat," he said when he had regained his balance. "Does it go down this fast, too?"

"You'll never know," Lodgepoole reminded him.

After a couple minutes, the elevator stopped abruptly. The doors slid open and we were in the alley where I had found Lodgepoole and Al that morning. I took in a huge gulp of fresh air. It felt great to be out in the open again and to be able to see the sky. It seemed as though we'd been underground for days instead of just hours. It was only two-thirty.

Al brought out his tracker and switched it on. I peered over his shoulder and saw that the arrow pointed due west. "About a half mile," Al announced. "Down Main Street."

"Then let's be off," Lodgepoole said. The two men led the way out of the alley and down the street. Simon and I exchanged worried glances.

I stopped and signaled silently for Simon to wait. "I know we decided we'd go home as soon as we got above ground," I said. "But I just don't think that would be the responsible thing to do. There's no way these two are going to be able to round up all five criminals on their own."

"But on the other hand," Simon said. "If we leave now, we avoid getting shot at. . . ."

Up ahead Lodgepoole and Al had noticed that we were lagging behind. "Kids today," Al snapped. "Do you want to come with us or not?"

"Well, actually—" Simon began.

"There's no time for chatter," Lodgepoole interrupted. He and Al glanced uneasily at one another. "Come along."

"I think they really need us," I whispered to Simon.

He nodded reluctantly. "Okay," he said.

"But if there's any gunplay, I'm out of here."

As usual, there were a lot of people on the street, but nobody seemed to notice that Al and Lodgepoole were holding huge tranquilizer rifles. They walked cautiously, and every thirty seconds or so they'd suddenly spin around to make sure no one was following them. This didn't exactly help me maintain my cool, but I reminded myself that the weapons were only tranquilizer guns. If Al or Lodgepoole shot me or Simon accidentally, we'd probably just have some really wild dreams.

We passed a row of shops at the edge of town and came up to an empty lot overgrown with trees and shrubs. Lodgepoole stopped and held his finger to his lips. "The signal is strong," he whispered. "All five of them must be in there together."

"Maybe it's an ambush," I suggested.

"Good thinking, kid." Al rubbed his chin. "Lodgepoole, we'd better split up. In precisely five mintues, you'll go in from here." To me and Simon he added, "You two follow me, but stay back. I'm going in from the other side of the lot to see if I can't get them from behind. If anything goes wrong, you two run and call the police." He held out his wrist. "Synchronize watches. It's two-forty-eight . . . now!"

I nodded, checking my own watch. Lodgepoole, pale and shaking, took a deep breath and then nodded. He held his rifle in hands that were starting to get slick with sweat. I couldn't blame him. Going into a wooded lot after five dangerous criminals wasn't exactly doing wonders for my stomach. I felt cold and queasy as I stooped down as low as I could and followed Al to the other side of the lot. I could hear Simon's footsteps right behind me.

We reached the far side of the lot and checked our watches. "Two minutes to go," Al whispered. "Now, stay low, stay behind me, and don't do anything stupid. They won't even have a chance to shoot. So just stay quiet."

"Okay," I agreed. The lot was thick with trees and odd-looking overgrown ferns that reached way above my head. I couldn't see more than ten feet into the lot.

There was a flash of movement, and I felt my shoulders tense up. Then I realized that it wasn't a person, but a dragonfly zipping through the air.

"It's time," Al announced softly. "Come on."

It was too late to back out now.

I stuck close behind Al, who was following a pathway of trampled grass and weeds through the trees.

"Did you hear that?" Simon suddenly whispered.

"Hear what?" I asked. A shiver ran up my spine.

"Listen."

We had lost sight of Main Street, and even the noise of the cars vanished. All that I could hear was the faint breeze in the leaves and birds chirping and singing overhead.

Then I heard it. Something was moving beside us along the path. It was making a gentle rustling sound as it tracked us through the trees.

"Al, I think there's someone in there," I whispered, pointing off the path to our right.

Al listened for a moment. "Probably just a dodo," he declared.

And then, suddenly, we saw movement in the bushes. Al whipped the rifle around and fired.

We heard a gasp and Lodgepoole came stumbling out onto the path. A bright green dart bounced off his arm and he collapsed onto a pile of dead leaves.

"Oh, my," Al exclaimed. He looked down at his tracking device, then wildly around, and finally up into the trees. "According to this, they're supposed to be right here. But I can't see them anywhere at all." He scanned the area again. "And then there's Lodgepoole. . . ."

"Is he going to be okay?" Simon asked anxiously.

"Sure," Al replied. He took a small bottle from his pocket. "The last time we used the guns, he managed to shoot himself in the foot. I always keep a supply of antidote around for emergencies like this one."

"Shot himself in the foot?" Simon asked. "I thought you guys were supposed to be professionals."

"Well, we are," said Al. "But everyone makes mistakes. Surely you know that." He waved the bottle under Lodgepoole's nose.

"Come on, sleeping beauty. Time to wake up."

Lodgepoole gave a strangled yelp, and coughed as his eyes blinked open. He sat bolt-upright, and looked around. "What happened?" he asked, feeling his chest for wounds. "Did they get me?"

"No, no," Al answered. "I got you by mistake. They got away."

"I can't feel my feet," Lodgepoole said. "They're completely numb." He started to wiggle his ankles around wildly. Then I noticed something in the bushes by his feet.

I went closer and uncovered a pile of shoe boxes. I picked up the top one and lifted the lid.

Inside lay a pair of battered cowboy boots.

"Um, I think I know what the problem is," I announced. I held up one boot. "They've found the tracking devices. And they probably bought themselves some new shoes."

"Oh, terrific," Al grumbled. He thrust the tracking device into his pocket. "Now what do we do?"

Lodgepoole clambered unsteadily to his feet.

"We split up and look for them," I said. "They've changed shoes, but there's no other clothing here. So they're still wearing their regular clothes. Three cowboys, a sea captain, and a guy wearing a parachute. How hard can it be to spot them?"

"Especially since they think you've lost them," Simon agreed. "They'll probably be getting a false sense of security by now."

"But they could be anywhere," Lodgepoole protested. "It's a big town."

"Wherever they are they're probably planning their next crime," I said. "I don't know how they paid for the shoes, but they're probably pretty broke by now. So we know that what they need is cash."

"Marshall's right," Simon agreed. "Let's check the banks."

"I'll check out the Bank of Eerie and you check out Eerie Savings and Loan," I said to Simon.

"What about us?" Lodgepoole asked. He had sat down again and was still wiggling his feet around.

"Why don't you two just take it easy for a little while?" I suggested. "Get your strength back. If we find those guys, you'll need to be ready to rush right over with the tranquilizers." I knew how much pride they both took in their jobs, but it seemed as though the only way we could possibly make any progress would be with them on the sidelines—at least for a little while.

Al's face broke into a huge grin and he sat down immediately on a log. "Great idea!" he exclaimed. "We'll be waiting."

"Okay, Simon," I said. "It's you and me."

6

*O*n my way to the Bank of Eerie I ran past World of Stuff and I realized how hungry I was. Unlike Lodgepoole and Al, I really did want to handle the situation in a professional way, so I decided to stop for a late lunch.

The store was more crowded than usual but I was in a hurry. I almost interrupted Mr. Radford waiting on some customers at a booth in the corner, but something about them made me stop and wait. They were talking in loud voices and acting as if they had never had ice cream before. Two of them were wearing dusty old cowboy hats. All of a sudden it dawned on me. I had stumbled across the missing Missing People.

Quickly I crouched down behind a display shelf and scrambled as close to them as I could get.

One of them was wearing a tan suede vest with fringes and a large-brimmed hat. "What do you call this again?" he asked, tapping his dish with his spoon.

Mr. Radford beamed happily at his five new customers. "Pistachio almond fudge," he replied. "You like it, Mr. um . . . ?"

"Cassidy," the man said. "But you can go right ahead and call me Butch. Best thing I've eaten in years. I've a hankering to try something with butterscotch next."

"Coming right up," Mr. Radford promised, heading back to the counter.

One of the men at the booth spoke with a thick accent, and I knew he was the Dutchman. He slurped down another spoonful. "We never had food like this," he declared. "This iced cream is magnificent. Don't you think so Jesse?"

"Better than any I ever tasted," Jesse James agreed.

Suddenly my stomach rumbled. I jumped back and held my breath, my heart pounding in my ears.

Butch Cassidy laughed. "Sounds like someone around here is still hungry," he said. He looked around the group. "'Fess up, was that you, D.B.?"

Another man wearing a parachute wrapped around his shoulders scowled. "Heck, no," said D.B. "It must have been the Sundance Kid. But don't we have more important stuff to talk about than food?"

"Right now," Sundance commented, "food is uppermost on my mind. Hey, I've slept away the whole century. My stomach wants some attention and I aim to please it— which this ice cream sure does. How about something with strawberries?" he called out.

"You got it!" Mr. Radford called back.

"We should be making plans," D.B. insisted. "The five of us together can outwit the police in this hick town."

"But do they have anything worth stealing?" Butch said. "I've only seen two banks. And from the way that the store-man's eyes gleamed when I paid him in gold, it doesn't look like they get to see much of it around here."

"That's true," D.B. agreed reluctantly.

"So what do they use for money?" asked the Dutchman.

"Mostly slips of paper," D.B. explained. He pulled a note from his pack and showed it to the others.

"I prefer the feel of silver myself," Jesse James scoffed. "This paper stuff don't seem like real money to me. I like my cash to have some weight to it. Don't they use silver or gold anymore?"

"Most of it's kept in reserves," D.B. explained. "It's not used for common trans-actions."

"Then it seems to me," Butch said, "that these reserves are what we should hit." He stopped talking as Mr. Radford brought over another round of ice cream. "Say, do you have some sort of local newspaper here?"

"Local?" The storekeeper nodded, and fetched him one from the rack. "The *Eerie Examiner*," he explained. "All the news that's fit to print. And quite a bit that isn't. Enjoy, gentlemen!"

I was crouched behind a stack of comic books. I shuffled a bunch of them out of the way and leaned forward. If I could hear their plan, then I'd be able to tell Al and Lodgepoole where to catch them.

Mr. Radford returned to the counter and Butch Cassidy swallowed a huge spoonful of mint and butterscotch ice cream. Then he started to scan the news. After a few moments I saw him sit up sharply in the booth.

"Boys," he announced. A thin smile crept over his lips. "I think I've found us our opportunity." He pushed the page he'd been reading into the center of the table. "Take a look at this."

"What is it?" the Dutchman asked. "I can speak English, but my reading is not so good."

"Well," Butch Cassidy began. "There's going to be a special train running through this here town of Eerie tomorrow. It's going to be carrying a whole load of gold bullion from one of those reserves that D.B. here was talking about. And there's going to be plenty of passengers, too." His grin widened. "Now, it seems to me that this is exactly the kind of opportunity we're looking for."

"I'll say it is," Sundance agreed,

whistling. "Ten million dollars in gold bullion," he read. "Even with the price of things these days, that's got to be worth stealing."

"Two million each," mused Jesse James. "Yes, sir, I have to agree with you there. That sounds like something worth going for. What do you reckon, D.B.?"

The hijacker nodded. "Two million each is a tidy sum. I'm in."

"And I also," agreed the Dutchman. "So—now we have our target. What we need next is a plan."

Just at that moment my stomach rumbled again, even more loudly than the last time. I jumped back and waited for a moment, but the criminals had been too excited about their plan to notice, so I crouched back into my spot.

"Agreed," Butch Cassidy was saying. "So I suggest that we finish our ice creams, and then see if we can hire ourselves some horses somewhere. I have to admit I'd love to drive one of these newfangled automobiles, but it looks to me like they might take some practice getting used to."

"I don't think you'll find horses," D.B.

told him. "They're not exactly common transport these days. But I can drive, and I think we can hire ourselves a van pretty cheap."

"All right, whatever you think is best," Butch said amiably. He polished off the last of his treat and then stood up. "Well, gentlemen, it looks as though by this time tomorrow, we're going to not only be free, but rich, too."

The other four stood up and left some coins on the table. Then they all walked toward the door.

"Bye!" Mr. Radford called cheerfully. "Be sure to come again."

"As long as you stock ice cream, you can bet we'll be back," Butch assured him.

I waited for a minute to make sure that they were gone. Then I jumped up from behind the comic book shelf and whipped out my walkie-talkie. I radioed Simon, Al, and Lodgepoole and told them to meet me at World of Stuff. My rumbling stomach was going to be a dead giveaway if I didn't get something to eat. And now that I knew their plan, I knew we had twenty-four hours to make up a plan of our own.

When Simon, Lodgepoole, and Al arrived at World of Stuff I filled them in on what I'd overheard.

"Why didn't you go after them?" Al asked.

I was too busy eating my french fries to answer right away. But after I'd finished chewing, I reminded Al that I wasn't carrying a tranquilizer gun, so there was really nothing I could do.

"You were right to call us in," Simon said. "There are too many of them to handle alone."

Lodgepoole lifted a forkful of coleslaw to his mouth. "Let's not forget that I am a Certified Misappropriation Engineer," he said. "I'll handle this."

Mr. Radford rushed over to our table. "How's everything? Can I get you anything else?" he asked.

"No, thanks. We're fine," I said.

But Lodgepoole interrupted. "What we need now are the facts," he said.

Mr. Radford looked confused. "Yes, of course," he said. "Coming right up." But he stayed right where he was next to our booth. He opened his mouth as if he was going to ask a question, but then he just shut it again without saying a word.

I said, "Lodgepoole just wants to ask you some questions, Mr. Radford."

Mr. Radford smiled. "No problem," he said. "What did you need to know?"

"Did you by any chance see what direction those five men were headed in when they left?" asked Lodgepoole.

But even though I'd seen Mr. Radford wave to them from the door, he couldn't remember in which direction they'd been walking.

As we finished our meal, though, I remembered. "They were going to rent a van," I told the others.

"Do you think we should call the Head Office for backup?" Lodgepoole asked. His voice was quavering.

Al slammed a fist down on the table. "Absolutely not," he said. "Unless you want to be out of a job. Unless you want to be out on the street again."

Lodgepoole sniffed and a tear rolled down his cheek.

"Al, did you have to make him cry?" Simon asked.

I patted Lodgepoole on the shoulder. "Don't worry, Lodgepoole," I said. "We've got those guys covered." Now that I had some food in my stomach I was feeling a lot better about the whole thing.

Al said, "There's no need for us to call in the Head Office. Our friends here—" he pointed to me and Simon "—can keep an eye on them to make sure they stay out of trouble while we get ready for tomorrow. I'm sure it's just a matter of checking the Bureau manual again. They have a plan for every emergency," he added.

"I'm not a sheriff," Lodgepoole insisted. "I've never had to deal with criminals before."

He had a point, but I didn't want to think about it since I'd only just then finished eating.

"You guys check that manual carefully," I said. "Simon and I will follow Butch Cassidy and the others. We'll radio you if we have any news."

Before leaving World of Stuff, Simon and I made a few more purchases. We each bought a new pair of mirrored sunglasses and a newspaper. These would come in handy if we wanted to get close to the outlaws without being noticed. We headed directly over to Eerie Rentals.

And as soon as we arrived we spotted them. They were walking around the car lot, oohing and ahhing as if they'd never seen a sports car before—which I guess most of them hadn't. I put on my mirrored sunglasses and started walking around the lot, looking at the cars as though I was going to rent one. Simon did the same.

Butch Cassidy seemed the most excited of all the men. "Have you tried sitting in one of them vehicles?" he asked. "The seats are sure soft on the caboose."

"Never mind that," D.B. pointed out. "These cars are fast! We'll have no problem making our getaway."

"I got to admit," Butch said, "these modern times definitely have some fine things to recommend them. I'm going to have to learn me how to drive one of these here automobiles."

"A guy could get used to this," Jesse James agreed. "A lot more comfy than riding a horse. And I love that music-making box they've got in this thing. Fancy being able to make music without no people and no instruments!"

"Yes, sir," Sundance commented. "I could take a powerful liking to this era. Especially when Butch finishes coming up with a plan for us to become real wealthy. How's it going, Butch?"

"Pretty good," Butch admitted modestly. He pointed to a place on the map he was holding. "There's got to be someplace up here where we can force the train to stop, and then we can figure out the rest of it."

The others crowded around him as he traced a line with his finger on the map. "See this here river?" he said. "This just might be our spot. A train crossing a river usually means a bridge."

I knew the spot he was talking about, where the railroad crossed the Eerie River.

"Gentlemen," he said. "This here's our opportunity. All we have to do is to block the rail on the bridge and force the train to come to a halt. Then we can rob it at our leisure."

"And how do we make our getaway?" asked D.B.

"By water," Butch replied. "We stop the train on the bridge and lower the bullion down to a boat on the river. Dutchman, that would be your responsibility. You think you can get us a boat?"

The Dutchman nodded emphatically. "There's never been a boat I couldn't handle. And I'll be able to find one down at the wharf. This little town is so small, so innocent, someone will probably give me a boat to borrow. I won't even have to steal one."

"Great," Butch said. "So we stop the train and lower the gold to the boat. All we need is some way down ourselves. We could go down the ropes we use to lower the gold, but that seems a mite risky."

D.B. grinned at this. "Boys," he announced, "what we need are parachutes." He tapped the one he wore on his back. "It's how I bailed out of a plane and made my last getaway. All you do is jump, and pull the cord. The chute comes out of the pack and drops you down, light as a feather, onto the boat."

Sundance admired the pack. "Gee, we really could have done with a couple of these that time we jumped off a cliff, Butch."

"Yeah. I can remember a few jumps I've taken where it would have been mighty nice to land gently. Will it be hard for you to find some more of these here parachutes?" he asked D.B.

"Not at all," the hijacker answered. "I spotted some at that store where we had our ice cream. I can go back and pick them up right now, along with anything else we might need."

Butch thought for a moment. "A couple of hefty saws might help," he said. "I'm thinking that we should just drop a couple of trees. We can use that van to haul them into place to block the bridge."

"Not saws," D.B. said with a grin. "Chain saws. Those suckers will do the work in no time and with less effort."

Sundance smiled again. "Like I keep saying, I really am taken with this here era. Hey, life is easy. Especially for us train robbers. This is sure going to be fun."

Butch nodded. "And tomorrow it will be profitable fun." He grinned. "*Very* profitable. Now, let's go rent us a vehicle."

Simon nudged me in the elbow as the men started to walk into the rental place. "C'mon," he whispered. "We've got to find out what kind of car they'll be driving."

We stood at the entrance to the lot and waited. Finally we saw a gray minivan pull out. I could see the men inside it and I could hear them laughing as they drove away.

"They made a sensible choice," Simon said. "A good family car."

The tires squealed as the van sped around a corner. "I just hope Al and Lodgepoole have come up with a really good plan," I said. Simon and I looked at each other.

"Or maybe we should think of something," Simon suggested.

I nodded. We radioed Al and Lodgepoole to meet us outside the rental lot. We had overnight to come up with a way to stop Butch Cassidy, the Sundance Kid, and three other legendary crooks. Deep down inside, I had to admit to myself that the odds of us catching those guys weren't too good. And the odds of us getting away unharmed—well, I decided not to think about it.

"Well, at least we know things can't get much worse," I said.

It's amazing how wrong you can be sometimes.

7

I had thought things couldn't possibly get any worse after losing five very dangerous crooks in my own hometown. But they could get worse. And that's what was about to happen.

"Surprise!" said a familiar voice.

I turned around to see Dash watching us, a wide grin on his face.

"Oh, no," I groaned.

It's not exactly that I don't like Dash. Sometimes he can be helpful. It's just that Dash operates on his own agenda and by his own rules. And for the most part, neither of them coincide with what I want or with the what's legal. Dash will do anything to get what he wants. He'll even lie or cheat or steal. It just doesn't bother him.

I like to think of Dash as one more strange thing about Eerie. For example, he's only a few years older than I am, but he has the gray hair of an old man. He wears a trench coat that's about three sizes too big for him and he hides stolen food and other things inside it. He lives alone in a shack in the woods, and is generally pretty antisocial.

Except when he's up to something. So you can see how running into Dash was not good news.

"What do you want?" I demanded.

Grinning even wider, he moved closer to us. "You two look like you've lost something," he said. "I've been following you around for the last twenty minutes. You were looking for something, and now you've found it. But you don't like what you've found, do you? I figured you might need my help. For a price, of course."

At that moment, Lodgepoole and Al strode into sight. They hurried over to Simon and me, and I explained what Dash had just said.

"We're not interested," Lodgepoole said quickly. He nudged me with his elbow. "Tell him we're not interested."

"Well, that's the problem," I had to confess. "I mean, if there's anyone who might be able to help us, it's Dash."

"That's right," Dash agreed. "I know everything that's going on in this town, and for a price I can tell you what I know."

"It's out of the question," Al hissed. "We can't tell anyone else."

"About the Bureau of Lost?" asked Dash.

"Who told you about that?" Lodgepoole gasped. He turned to me. "You must have!" he said accusingly.

"I did not," I replied honestly.

"He's telling the truth," Dash added. "I make it my business to know things, just like you make it your business to lose things." He snapped his fingers. "Got it! You've lost something you're not supposed to have, and now you're looking for it."

Lodgepoole had gone almost green at the thought of someone else knowing about his Bureau. But what Dash was saying was interesting me. Dash had his own secrets and his own resources. He obviously already knew what was going on, and he might just be able to help us catch the missing men. If Lodgepoole and Al agreed.

"I think it's worth taking a chance," I told them. "Dash is almost as crooked as the men we're after. If anyone can figure out how to stop them, it's him."

"Thanks," said Dash. "I think."

"Besides," I added, "we aren't having any luck on our own, and it's your jobs that are on the line here."

Lodgepoole threw up his hands in despair. "Oh, very well. Tell him! Tell the whole world, for all I care! I'm just giving up!"

I turned to Dash. "Do you know about the Bureau of Missing?"

"All those guys frozen in tubes like ice cream cones? Sure." He grinned again. "You've lost one of them, haven't you?"

"Actually, five of them." I explained the whole thing to him.

Dash whistled in appreciation of our problem. "And you have to get these guys back fast? Hey, without me to help you, your chances would be zero." He turned back to Lodgepoole. "But it'll cost you."

Lodgepoole sniffed. "I could tell you were

the mercenary sort. Very well, what's your price?"

Dash shook his head. "It's not money. I happen to have lost something very valuable. And I'd like it back."

Al stomped his foot impatiently. "Why does everyone keep expecting us to *return* things?" he demanded. "That's not the idea, not the idea at all." He sulked for a moment, and then sighed. "What is it you've lost?"

"My memory," Dash answered. All Dash knew about his past was that he'd woken up one morning in Eerie, Indiana—with no idea who he was or how he'd gotten there.

Lodgepoole smiled. "Well, we can't help you there. We deal only in physical items. Whoever took your memory, it wasn't the Bureau of Lost. So I can't give it back." He looked very relieved.

"In that case," Dash answered cheerfully, "I'll settle for cash. Cold, hard cash. A thousand dollars."

"A *thousand* dollars?" Al squeaked. "We can't pay you that much!"

"Then there's no deal," Dash replied. "Catch them yourself." He gave me a grin.

"Good luck, sheriff." He started to turn away.

"Wait!" Lodgepoole looked very ill. "All right, it's a deal. You'll get your thousand dollars—*if* you can help us."

"Oh, I can help, all right. What we need to do first is get into the criminal mindset." Dash grinned again. "You know that they went to World of Stuff, right?"

"Yeah, we already know that," I said. "They had ice cream there and read the paper."

"And they're planning on stopping back there for parachutes and chain saws, right?" he continued.

I nodded.

"Well let's move it!" he exclaimed. "We'll need to be even better equipped than they are. World of Stuff, here we come."

I hesitated for a second. This was the great idea that Dash was charging a thousand dollars for? It wasn't exactly Einstein's theory of relativity. Still, Dash seemed pretty confident. And right now, that was a lot more than I could say for the rest of us.

A moment later I was running along

after the others in the direction of World of Stuff.

Soon the five of us were standing outside the store, peering in through the large window, looking for the five crooks.

Mr. Radford's face beamed back at us. "See anything you like?" he asked. Aside from him, the store was empty.

"We're not sure," Lodgepoole said with a sigh.

I went into the store, the others following me. "Mr. Radford, remember those five new customers we were talking about?"

"Sure do." He gave me another grin, and showed me a solid silver dollar. "Paid me really nicely, and ate tons of ice cream."

"Have they been back here?" I asked.

"They sure were," Mr. Radford said. "I had a feeling they were going to be regulars. One of them came back about ten minutes ago and bought some parachutes. Just got them in, too, and sold them like that." His eyebrows rose. "Do you fellows want to buy some? I've still got some left."

"It would probably be a pretty good idea," Dash said. "They might come in handy tomorrow."

Just then the door swung open and D.B. Cooper walked right up to the counter. "Hi, there," he said to Mr. Radford. "When I was buying those parachutes a few minutes ago I forgot that I also need a couple of chain saws. Do you have any in stock?"

"Quick, hide," I hissed to the others. They scattered to the back of the store and disappeared behind the shelves. I started to inch away.

But Mr. Radford called out to me, "Hey, Marshall, here's one of the guys you've been asking about. If you have so many questions about what they're buying, why don't you ask him yourself?"

D.B. swung his head around sharply. "Asking about me?" he said. Then he saw my face. "Hey, you were in that rental lot. You've been following me around. What do you think you're doing?"

I felt the blood drain from my face and I froze.

D.B. Cooper lunged for me, but I jumped out of his reach just in time. My heart was pounding in my throat as I raced toward the door and out onto the street.

I looked around wildly for a place where

I could take cover, and then dashed around to the alley behind the store. There was a huge Dumpster there filled with trash. Without a moment's hesitation, I scrambled into it.

D.B.'s footsteps pounded out into the alley. Then they stopped. I could hear him pacing around, muttering under his breath. "Where is that kid, where is that kid," he was saying.

I realized that I was holding my breath and I slowly exhaled. That was a mistake. Because it meant that the next thing I'd have to do would be to inhale. And when you're sitting on a stack of week-old garbage, that's never a good idea. A foul stench filled the air and I could feel a tickling sensation in my nostrils.

The sound of D.B.'s footsteps started to fade away. And then I sneezed.

In an instant the man was peering over the edge of the Dumpster. "Ugh," he gasped when he took in the smell. He reached one long arm over the side and grabbed me by the shoulder.

My legs shaking, I climbed back out and stood before him in the deserted alley.

"You'd better have a darn good explanation for this," D.B. began. He was squeezing my shoulder painfully.

"I—I—I do have an explanation," I stuttered. "I didn't mean to bother you. It's just for a school project," I said.

D.B. Cooper squinted down at me. "School project?" he asked.

Luckily an idea had popped into my head and I quickly continued. "Yes, sir. I'm doing a project about the Eerie tourist industry," I said. "I noticed that you seemed to be a visitor, so I was trying to figure out where you spend your money. I'll report what you bought back to my teacher," I explained.

D.B. let go of my shoulder. "You'd better not report anything. Do you understand? I'm not a tourist," he said. Then he chuckled. "You might say I'm here on . . . business. So you stop following me around. Understand?"

"Absolutely," I answered. "No problem. Thanks for your help." I began to edge away toward the street.

"And if I catch you or your little friend following me again you'll be sorry," he called out after me.

About ten minutes later, as soon as my pulse had returned to normal, I sat down on a bench in front of the Bank of Eerie and radioed Simon. He and the others had watched from the back of World of Stuff while D.B. returned and bought some chain saws, then drove away. They were waiting for me at the store.

"I don't ever want to look into that guy's face again," I said. "What we need is a brilliant plan."

"Do you have one?" Lodgepoole looked at Dash hopefully.

"Not yet," he admitted. "I'm still mulling the clues over in my mind. But we've got all night. I'm sure that by tomorrow morning one of us will have thought of something really good."

I just wished that I was as confident as Dash. But as I slowly walked toward home, I couldn't forget what D.B. had said. If we messed this one up, we sure *would* be sorry.

8

*B*y the next morning, I was almost frantic. I'd spent the whole evening with Simon, trying to work out a plan. And we'd had absolutely no luck. I was distracted the next morning at breakfast, but in my house that's not something that really gets noticed. Dad's always thinking about his work, and Mom's always planning the day's activities for her party-planning store at the mall. As for my sister, Syndi— well she's a total space cadet.

When I poured orange juice into my bowl of cereal, Mom just asked if that's what kids were eating these days.

"No, Mom. I just like to try new things," I said. I dumped the whole mess into the trash. I was too upset to eat, anyway.

"Aren't you going to eat anything at all?" Mom asked.

"I'm meeting Simon at World of Stuff later and I don't want to be too full," I said.

Mom looked confused, but then she smiled. "Okay, Marshall, just as long as you don't start making a habit of skipping breakfast. It's the most important meal of the day, you know."

So Sunday breakfast went off pretty much as usual. But no matter how hard I thought, I couldn't come up with a plan at all. Simon came over after breakfast. I didn't need to ask him if he'd thought of anything once I saw the expression on his face. And he didn't bother asking me, either.

"Maybe Dash has come up with something," he suggested. "Or Al or Lodgepoole." But I could see he was just trying to cheer me up. Inside, he was just as scared as I was.

That's the problem with inspiration. When it doesn't happen, there's not much you can do about it. Still, Dash was being paid for this, and he'd seemed so confident. I hoped that he'd come through for us.

We'd arranged to meet the others at nine o'clock at World of Stuff. When we arrived I still wasn't feeling too hungry, so I just ordered a plain grilled cheese sandwich.

"The old brain's not working too well, huh?" Mr. Radford asked sympathetically. He didn't have a clue as to what was worrying us, but we preferred it that way.

"Not working at all," I admitted. "Thanks for the grilled cheese, though. Maybe it'll kick-start some ideas."

"Can't hurt," Mr. Radford agreed cheerfully. "Ah! More customers!" He scurried off to get more place settings as Lodgepoole and Al arrived. And a second later, Dash walked into the store.

They sat down with us, and I haven't seen four longer faces in Eerie since the time that Bigfoot accidentally ate one of Santa's reindeer.

"Look," Dash said finally, playing with the straw in his drink, "I did come up with an idea. But you might not like it. I'm not usually the type who would suggest something like this, but . . . Well, maybe we should just tell the police about this robbery."

"No!" chorused Al and Lodgepoole together. "They're bound to ask questions, and they're not going to like the answers they hear," Lodgepoole added.

"Is that all you could come up with?" Al asked. "The crooks know how to get into the Bureau of Lost. If they should tell the authorities, we'll be put out of business."

"And if they see the Bureau of Missing," Lodgepoole finished, "they might jump to the wrong conclusions and think that we're *kidnappers*."

"Well, you are," Simon pointed out. "And thieves."

Lodgepoole looked shocked. "We're nothing of the kind!" he exclaimed in horror. "We're duly Certified Misappropriation Engineers. We're career workers, not criminals."

"I guess it all depends on your point of view," I told them. "But you're right. We should only call in the police as a last resort. The problem is, there's five of them—all ruthless criminals, armed with guns. There's just the five of us. Two Certified Misappropriation Engineers, two school kids, and a dropout. With two tranquilizer guns. We're outclassed."

"But these guys are ancient," Simon protested. "We're modern kids in a modern world. We should have some advantages."

For the first time in twenty-four hours I felt a real ray of hope. "Simon," I said slowly, "I think you've got something. These guys might be criminal masterminds, but they're way out of date."

"Right! They're at least a century out of date," Dash said. "We'll crush them with our technology. We've got to be tons smarter than they are."

"Except for D.B. Cooper," Lodgepoole pointed out. "He's only about twenty-five years out of date."

"Then we have to use stuff that's after his time," I replied. I glanced around the store. "We need the technological edge. I wonder what Mr. Radford's got in stock recently."

"Let's go see," Dash said. "There's got to be *something* to give us an idea."

"There had better be," Al grumbled. "Because the train is scheduled to cross the bridge in just two hours."

A plan was finally forming in my head.

And World of Stuff was going to be our greatest resource. I consulted with Mr. Radford while the others finished their breakfasts. As always, he had exactly what we needed. He's really gifted in that way. He always knows what the new trends are going to be before anyone else, kind of like Madonna, only more so. Like those parachutes he'd just gotten in the day before. And the stuff he had for us now.

We were short on time, but Lodgepoole was kicking up a stink about paying. "I won't do it," he declared, trying to look firm. "I can't keep raiding the Bureau funds like this! How will I manage to hide it from management?"

"I don't care how," I told him. "Isn't it easier to explain away a few thousand dollars than five Missing People?"

"If you put it like that—" Lodgepoole began.

"If you remember, *I* am in charge right now," Al interrupted. "I'll authorize the expenditure as an emergency non-budgeted overrun. We'll figure out how to explain it later."

Lodgepoole sighed. "It will be on your

head," he said. "I'm having nothing to do with it."

"Of course not," Al agreed sarcastically. "You've only paid a thousand dollars to *him*." He gestured at Dash.

"For his help in apprehending the Missing People," Lodgepoole pointed out. He glanced at me. "He *is* going to help out, isn't he?"

"Definitely," I promised. I gestured to one of the items that I'd set aside at the front counter. "That's for him."

But Dash took one look at it and shook his head. "Oh, no," he said, crossing his arms firmly. "You're not getting me up in that."

Simon examined the hang glider kit with interest. "This looks cool," he decided. "I'll give it a try."

"Sorry, Simon," I told him. "There's no time for you to get the hang of it. But Dash already knows how to hang glide. I mean, he's always saying how he knows everything and has done everything. That includes hang gliding, right?" I asked.

"Well, yeah," Dash admitted, looking a little sheepish. "I've done some hang gliding. And that's why I know I'm not going up in one again."

"You're the only one who has gliding experience," I pointed out. "That means it has to be you."

"No way," he insisted.

I gave Lodgepoole a significant look, and he caught on immediately. With a wide grin, he turned to Dash. "How'd you like to lose that thousand dollars? It's surprising how much change can just . . . disappear."

Dash winced. I could tell that losing the money would really hurt. Greed and fear were battling for control of Dash. As I expected, greed won pretty easily.

"Okay," he growled. "I'll do it. But I won't like it."

"I don't really care whether you like it or not," I told him. "Just as long as you do it. We'll get you a walkie-talkie so that you can stay in touch with us on the ground. It'll be a cinch. You'll see." I turned to Lodgepoole and Al. "Now, you two both know what you've got to do, right?"

"Sure, kid, sure," Al said. "We've been over it already. We hire a minibus to get us all out there." He tapped his tranquilizer gun. "And we're armed and ready for action. Are the two of you ready?"

"Ready, willing, and eager," I assured him with a grin. "Butch Cassidy and his friends may think that they're pulling off the crime of the century, but I'm willing to bet that it's going to be the flop of the century by the time we're done with them."

"You'd better be right, kid," Al said. "Otherwise we're going to be out much more than a few thousand dollars in pocket change. We're going to be out of our jobs, and those five crooks are going to be out having the time of their lives." He gave me a significant look. "And if I'm fired, I can promise you that the rest of your life is going to be thoroughly miserable."

Well, that's *encouraging*, I thought sarcastically. Still, I wasn't too worried. Because now I had a plan. And it was going to work.

It just had to.

9

We rented a big green minibus and Al drove us all out to toward the railroad crossing. But as we passed the train station, we noticed that a huge crowd had gathered. We pulled off the road and Simon and I got out to investigate.

"I'm sure the Missing People have been spotted. Now the Bureau will find out about this for sure," Lodgepoole moaned.

"Don't jump to any conclusions," I cautioned. "We'll know for sure in a minute."

Simon and I made our way to the front of the crowd and peered into the station. What I saw was pretty weird.

There was a train stopped there, but it wasn't a normal one. Suddenly I remembered a notice I'd seen in the newspaper the day before. The train line was planning a Wild West Festival. And it was set for today!

They'd found an old steam engine that still worked, and some old railroad cars from the turn of the century. One of the cars was encased in an armored shell, and I knew that that was the one which held the gold.

A whole bunch of railroad enthusiasts had shown up to take a ride on the historic train. Several people were even dressed in period costume. A lot of the men wore cowboy hats, suede britches, and old-fashioned riding boots. The women were wearing long hoop skirts and were carrying parasols.

The driver and engineer were both dressed like rejects from Frontierland, with bib-fronted jeans and huge, floppy hats on their heads. The guards wore old-fashioned waistcoats and pocket watches on gold chains. Many of them had pasted false moustaches to their upper lips. The bullion train looked like something out of a John Wayne movie, and it was filled with innocent, unsuspecting passengers way too involved with themselves to notice anything else.

If you ask me, they all looked ridiculous. But they seemed to be happy enough about it, so who am I to complain? Except for one thing.

"How are we going to recognize the outlaws?" Simon asked.

"Don't worry," I said. "They'll be the ones holding up the train."

The train didn't stay long in the Eerie station. The engineer began to shovel loads of coal into the engine of the locomotive. Sweat was pouring down his face and he looked angry. I figured that this was probably his least favorite day of the year. And he didn't even know the danger he was in.

Soon the train had pulled out of the station and was steaming down the track towards the next town.

"Quickly, get back to the minibus," I shouted. Simon and I ran back to the bus and slammed the doors shut behind us.

Al revved the engine and we sped down the road.

"I can see the train," Simon said. He was hanging his head out the window, watching as it made its way along the track beside the road.

In our minibus we were making much better time than the old steam engine.

"It's going to be late," Dash said. "That will probably make Butch Cassidy and his gang pretty nervous. So watch out ahead. A nervous crook is an unhappy crook, and an unhappy crook is a gun-happy crook."

"We'd better pull over here," I said. We had reached a bend in the road, and just around the other side was the railroad bridge and the Eerie River. I knew that the outlaws would be waiting there. We all scrambled out of the minibus and crouched along the side of the road.

I heard the train screeching to a halt on the tracks. It had reached the bridge and I could see that the rails on the bridge had been blocked by very thick logs. The train whistle blasted and I could hear the rising voices of the people inside. They hadn't planned on a stop just outside of Eerie, Indiana.

Suddenly Butch Cassidy stepped out from behind some shrubs. He was holding a gun in each hand. But before he could do anything, the armored car holding the gold bullion opened up, and two of the guards looked out, confused.

"Is this some kind of a gimmick?" one of them asked.

"Why weren't we told about it?" asked the other.

Butch stuck his pistol into the first man's face. "This isn't a stunt," he said cheerfully. "It's a holdup. And since I'm holding the gun, you're the ones getting robbed. Do you catch my drift?"

Sundance and the others jumped forward and ran towards the stalled train.

"Is this a joke?" the second guard asked. "Because it's not funny."

Butch fired a single shot into the air. "Let's all just try to get along, shall we?" he said. "Why don't you two gentlemen begin unloading the gold, okay?"

I nudged Dash with my foot. "Go," I whispered.

"I told you," he whispered back. "I really hate hang gliding. I don't want to go."

My blood froze. The whole plan depended on this, and if Dash refused to help, we were sunk.

"Dash, we're counting on you," I said. "If you don't do this, Lodgepoole and Al will see to it that none of us ever find anything again. And don't forget about the money involved," I added.

Dash sighed. Then he rose and made his way back to the minibus to get the hang glider. From here on in, he'd be on his own.

Meanwhile, Jesse James had strode over to the passenger car. "Ladies and gentlemen," he called out. "I apologize for your unscheduled stop." He whisked a cowboy hat off the head of one of the male passengers. "Please place all your valuables in this hat, and know that you are contributing to a worthy cause—namely, me!" He let out a deep, throaty laugh.

One by one the passengers stepped out of the train and dropped their valuables into the hat. "Isn't this fun!" one lady exclaimed. "We not only reenact a train ride, but also a train robbery. I must say, this train line knows how to entertain." She pulled off a pair of earrings and a diamond wedding ring and dropped them into the hat. "I assume these will be returned to us at the next station," she said.

"Sure, ma'am," Jesse James responded. "You go ahead and assume whatever you want."

It was time for us to make our move. "It's now or never," I whispered.

"This had better work," Al growled.

"It will," I assured him. "Modern-day technology against the old West. Not even a competition, really." But I could feel the goose bumps rising on the backs of my arms. I turned to Al and Lodgepoole. "You two go down and deal with the Flying Dutchman. He'll be with their getaway boat on the river. Simon and I are giving you five minutes, so hurry."

"We know the plan," Al snapped. He and Lodgepoole had loaded their tranquilizer guns. They ran down the steep bank that led to the riverbed.

As soon as they were out of view Simon asked, "Do you think they'll be able to do it?"

I knew what he meant. They weren't the most efficient people we'd ever met.

"Even *they* can't mess this one up," I said. "The plan is so simple, it just has to work."

I glanced up at the sky. "And the same goes for Dash," I added.

I picked up my walkie-talkie just to check. "Dash, are you there?" I called softly.

"Where else would I be?" Dash's voice crackled over the radio in response. "I've circled around here about twelve times and I'm starting to get really dizzy. Should I come down now?" he asked hopefully.

"Not yet," I answered. "In a few more minutes we'll all be in position. Just hang on a little longer."

I signed off and glanced at my watch. There were only a couple more minutes left to wait. I tapped my fingers nervously against the ground where I was crouching and watched what was happening on the bridge. I could see the open door of the armored car. Two men were loading the gold blocks on a plank that was attached to a pulley. They were going to lower the gold down below the bridge to the riverbank, where the outlaws had to be waiting.

"It's time," I told Simon. My voice sounded strange to me, high-pitched and quavering. We started forward, keeping down low and trying to stay hidden behind the bushes. I switched on my walkie-talkie. "Okay, Dash, come on down."

We crawled over to the train and along the length of it to the far end. Then we looked up into the sky and waited.

The hang glider was about twelve feet across and bright orange. It dropped rapidly downward.

At first Butch Cassidy was too busy lowering the gold to notice Dash and the hang glider. The gold was hanging about ten feet down off the bridge now, and the train engineer was working hard to lower it smoothly with the pulley, just as Butch had instructed him.

"What the deuce is that?" the Sundance Kid suddenly shouted.

Butch Cassidy looked in the direction that Sundance was pointing. He shook his head. "Beats me," he answered, squinting up into the sunlight. "Looks like some kid in a crazy flying contraption."

The words were barely out of his mouth when Dash came swooping toward the train. He was holding a chain saw and as he flew down past the blocks of gold, he reached out and cut the rope.

Butch and Sundance yelped in shock as they saw the gold fly off the plank and scatter into the river below.

I couldn't help grinning. My plan was working.

I could picture what was happening down below. The Dutchman would be stunned and running for cover. That's when Lodgepoole and Al would hit him with the tranquilizer darts.

Meanwhile, Butch and Sundance jumped off the train and waved their pistols in the air, trying to aim at Dash. Dash was speeding away in the hang glider, but I wasn't sure if he was out of range. We couldn't take the chance. My heart was racing as I stepped out of the bushes with Simon right behind me. We both clutched the weapons we'd selected from the World of Stuff behind our backs.

"Drop the guns, boys," I said. "It's the end of the line."

Butch Cassidy and the Sundance Kid whirled around. Butch was looking me squarely in the eyes, and I blinked.

"What is this—'Children's Day' or something?" Butch said. "You kids better get home before someone gets hurt."

Part of me wanted to follow his advice. Really badly.

10

I stood my ground. "Eerie, Indiana, is my home," I said. "You're the one who's lost, isn't that right?"

But Butch just laughed. "What's that you've got behind your back, boy?" he sneered. "A water pistol?"

"Got it in one," I told him, pulling up my water blaster.

Sundance laughed. "We aren't afraid of any water pistol, kid," he said.

I saw them fingering their pistols, and for a moment my courage failed me. Maybe this wasn't going to work after all.

Luckily, Simon stepped forward. "You *should* be afraid," he informed them.

We pulled the triggers of our weapons at the same instant and two powerful jets of water slammed into Butch and Sundance's faces. We were carrying backpacks that contained tanks of pressurized water, and now the water was blasting Butch and Sundance off their feet. In alarm, they pulled at the ripcords on their parachutes and jumped off the embankment. They floated slowly in midair down to the river, where Al and Lodgepoole were waiting. I hoped.

"There's no time to lose," I said breathlessly. "We've still got two more to go."

We glanced at the train. The passengers who had been sitting near the armored car were running away, but the people toward the front of the train had missed the commotion. They were milling around, waiting for the driver to make an announcement.

D.B. Cooper was standing next to the engineer, holding a pistol. A look of concern lined his forehead. I remembered what he had said to me in the alley and I shivered.

But Simon walked right up to him. "Hi, I'm doing a school project and I was wondering if you could tell me anything about this old steam engine," he began.

D.B. scowled deeply. "I thought I told your friend to lay off the school projects," he said. "What's the big idea?" While D.B. was nervously questioning Simon I snuck up behind him. If I hit him with my water blaster from just the right angle, I could send him rolling down the embankment toward the river.

I jumped forward and pulled the trigger. A stream of water flew out, crashing into D.B. Cooper. He stumbled backward, reaching around wildly with his arms, trying to regain his balance. But when he began to roll down the steep embankment, he pulled on his ripcord and released his parachute. Soon he, too, was floating gently downward. *Another one for Lodgepoole and Al*, I thought triumphantly.

The train engineer stared at us in astonishment.

"It's okay," I told him. "He's being taken care of right now. He'll be locked away for a long, long time." I didn't want to go into the details so I left it at that.

"We've got to go after Jesse James," Simon reminded me. "I saw him running into one of the cars at the back of the train."

"Jesse James?" the engineer asked.

"Um, a code name," I said. "Why don't you forget that you ever heard it?"

"You two look way too young to be working for the police," he persisted.

"We're not young," I said. "We just look young. We were recruited to lull the bad guys into making mistakes."

The engineer looked more confused than ever as we hopped on the train.

"Look," I said. "Can you make this train move backwards?"

He didn't look as though he'd bought my explanation, but I guess he trusted us because he began to stoke the engine with coal. "Will do," he answered. He put a hand on the throttle and then with his other hand pulled on a line that released the whistle. It howled, and with the huffing of steam and the grinding of wheels, the train began to slowly back away from the bridge.

As I'd expected, the instant the train began to move, Jesse James, realizing that something was going wrong, ran to the doorway and began to climb out of the car. As soon as he had reached the roof, I yelled for the engineer to stop the train.

Simon and I jumped off, then ran to the

back and blasted Jesse with our water blasters. He flew off the roof, and a moment later, we saw his parachute open.

I turned to look at Simon. "What do you think the chances are that Lodgepoole and Al have tranquilized all those guys?" he asked.

It was a question I'd been trying to put out of my mind. "Not so good," I admitted.

"So what do we do now?" Simon asked.

I shrugged my shoulders. "As I see it, we've done our best. We've practically handed the Missing People to Lodgepoole and Al on a silver platter. If this plan didn't work, I see no choice but to go to the police."

Simon agreed.

We crept cautiously along a road that twisted down to the river. "We could radio them on our walkie-talkies," Simon suggested.

I shook my head. "If any of the outlaws are down there untranquilized, it will clue them right in on Al and Lodgepoole's location," I said.

Gradually, the sounds of the voices of the confused passengers grew softer. I listened for Al or Lodgepoole's voice. All I could hear was the sound of the river and my own footsteps on the pavement, with Simon's trailing next to me.

Then I heard it. The low rumble of a vehicle. A moment later, the minibus rounded the bend. Al was driving it and he honked the horn when he saw us. He pulled over to the side of the road.

"Well?" I asked.

"Well, what?" he countered.

"Did you get them?" Simon demanded impatiently. "They all dropped in their parachutes. Did you see them?"

Al glanced at Lodgepoole and shook his head sorrowfully. "When will you kids understand that Lodgepoole and I are professionals?" he said. "Of course we got them. They're in the back."

I felt a wave of relief.

"See, there they are. Sleeping like little rats," Lodgepoole added. He rolled down his window so that we could look in and see. Sure enough, Butch Cassidy, the Sundance Kid, D.B. Cooper, Jesse James, and the Flying Dutchman were all snoring in the back of the minibus.

EPILOGUE

*A*s I'd expected, the authorities didn't believe most of what the train crew told them about the holdup. Butch Cassidy, Jesse James, and undercover midgets with water pistols just didn't make much sense to them. They assured the *Eerie Examiner* that they had leads, but I didn't worry about it. I knew that the secrets of the Bureau of Lost would continue to be safe.

Divers recovered almost all of the lost gold from the river, though a few blocks had to be reported missing. And Lodgepoole and Al were relieved to find that no sightings of the Missing People were reported in the gossip column.

I ran into Al on the street a couple days

later and he told me that he'd been demoted.

"Hey, I'm not much of a desk person, anyway," he said. "I'll leave that to Lodgepoole. Me, I prefer being out in the open air."

"Did Head Office find out what happened?" I asked.

"Not exactly," Al responded. "But they heard about the hullabaloo and guessed that something strange had happened. They said they wanted a more experienced man in the director position."

"And what about our request to meet them?"

"Request to meet them? Oh, yeah. Sorry, kid. Request denied. But I can guarantee that you'll never lose anything again. How's that?"

"That's the least they can do," I said. "So we're never going to get a decent explanation for all the cyrogenic people they've got down there?"

Al shrugged. "That information's on a 'need-to-know' basis," he said. "And you don't need to know."

When I left him he was heading over to

the coat check at the Eerie Theatre to collect sticks of chewing gum and tissues from people's coat pockets. Not my idea of a rewarding job, but he seemed happy enough.

That night, as Simon and I were finishing up our notes on the case to put in our Evidence Locker, I told him that I was far from satisfied.

"Is the Bureau planning to release any of the Missing People at any point? And if so, when?" I asked.

"Who knows?" Simon answered. Then he pulled a postcard out of his pocket. "But take a look at this. I found it in my closet. I think Al left it there for us."

He held it out. On it, in neat block letters was written: *Thanks for the holiday. Warmest regards, Amelia Earheart.*

*I*t all started with the statue of Zebediah Eerie. Actually it all started a little before that, in Miss Earhart's history class. We were talking about exploring. Miss Earhart had just finished telling us about how she'd spent the summer getting her pilot's license and taking some wild rides in her plane. Then she started talking about the ancient city of Atlantis. Atlantis is this city that some people believe sank right into the ocean thousands of years ago. No one really knows where it might have been, so no one has ever found the ruins. But all kinds of weird things were supposed to have happened there, which is why people are so interested in it.

"Atlantis was reported to be the center of many strange events," said Miss Earhart. "According to the little information we have about the city, all kinds of phenomena reportedly occurred there. One report talks about people changing into werewolves and mermaids. Another one claims that the Atlanteans could fly without machines."

I raised my hand. "Who were the Atlanteans?" I asked. "Where did they come from?"

"We don't really know," answered Miss Earhart. "Some people believe that Atlantis was created by aliens. In fact, it has even been suggested that the entire city was really a gigantic spaceship, and that it didn't sink into the ocean but flew up into the stars, taking everyone with it. But that's just a story, of course. We all know that aliens don't exist."

I could have told her a few things about aliens that might have made her change her mind about their existence, but I kept quiet about that. "Is there *any* proof that Atlantis ever existed?" I asked instead.

Miss Earhart shook her head. "Not really, Marshall," she said. "All we have to go on are some old manuscripts that mention the city. But none of them included maps, so we don't have a geographical location for it."

"So where do you think it is?" I asked.

"Well, I'm only an amateur explorer, so I can't really say. But I will tell you that I'm planning an expedition into the Bermuda Triangle over spring break to take a look around and see what's there."

The Bermuda Triangle. I'd read a lot about that in a book I'd found over the summer. The Bermuda Triangle is this really creepy part of the world where all sorts of weird stuff has happened. According to the book, a lot of ships and planes have disappeared without a trace while sailing or flying through the Bermuda Triangle. They just up and vanished into thin air, sometimes even while people were watching from other planes or ships. A lot of pilots who fly through there say that their navigational instruments all go crazy or stop working when the plane is in the Triangle. Some boat captains have reported that their ships are surrounded by very heavy fog for hours at a time, and that their ships' clocks actually run backwards as long as they're in the Triangle.

"Do you think Atlantis might be in the Bermuda Triangle?" I asked. If it were, that might explain all the strangeness that went on there.

Miss Earhart smiled. "I can't say for sure," she said. "But I do think they might possibly be connected."

Before she could continue telling us more about Atlantis, the bell rang for the end of the day. I gathered up my books and left, but I didn't stop thinking about Atlantis and the people who lived there. It was hard for me to believe that such a bizarre place had existed and that no one had written more about it. No one knew exactly where it was. How could something like that happen?

I was still imagining what Atlantis must have been like as I got my jacket from my locker and headed outside. When I pushed open the front door of the school, I saw Simon waiting for me on the steps.

"Hey," I said. "How was your day?"

Simon sighed. "Don't even ask," he said. "I'm never going to make it through algebra. And in gym, Mr. Ripley made us hang from the chin-up bar to see if we could grow any taller. He said the first kid whose feet reached the floor would get a part in some show he's doing. Man, is he weird."

"I remember that," I said. "Wait until he puts you in the locked trunk to see how long it takes you to get out."

"I can't wait. So how was your day? Any weirdness?"

"Not yet," I said. "But I've been thinking about something. What do you know about Eerie?"

"You mean besides the fact that it's the strangest place in the whole world?" said Simon.

"I know it's strange," I said. "But have you ever wondered *why* it's so strange? I mean, has it always been so weird, or is this something new?"

Simon thought for a minute. "I don't know," he said finally. "You're the only other person I've met who notices how strange it is. And now that you mention it, I don't really know anything about Eerie's history at all. I've never heard anybody talk much about it."

While we talked, we were moving along the main street of town. We were just coming to the town hall, a brick building that sat on a lawn of green grass. I'd been inside the place a couple of times, but I'd never noticed much about it except for the statue that stood on a pedestal in front of the building.

It was a statue of a man. He was dressed in uniform, like a soldier, and his face looked stern. When I looked more closely I could see that his military boots were a bit shinier than the rest of the statue.

I stopped in front of it. "For instance," I said to Simon. "Who's this guy? I've passed by this statue hundreds of times, but I have no idea who he is or why he's even here. What does he have to do with Eerie?"

Simon pointed to the base of the statue. "Why not just read the plaque?" he suggested. Good old Simon, always pointing out the obvious.

I knelt down and looked at the brass plate affixed near the statue's shiny boots. It was old, and it hadn't been cleaned in a long time. I had to rub a lot of dirt away before I could read the engraving.

"Zebediah Eerie," I read. "Founder of our beloved town."

That was it. There was nothing that said who exactly Zebediah Eerie was or what he'd done to get a whole town named after him.

"Maybe it's time we did a little investigating," I said. "I want to know more about this Zebediah Eerie and who he was."

"What good will it do to get the scoop on some old dead guy?" asked Simon. "It sounds like a homework assignment to me, and I have enough of that to do."

"It isn't just about Zebediah Eerie," I explained. "It's about this whole town. If we find out more about Zebediah, maybe we'll find out more about what's been happening here and why Eerie is so weird."